THE PLAYPEN

By

Donald Boone

THE PLAYPEN

STORIES FOR THE
BEDROOM

CHOOSING LOVERS

SEXUAL HAPPINESS

MEN & WOMEN: WHICH
ONE DO YOU WANT

INTRODUCTION

There comes the time when all of us can no longer function sexually in a manner of which we prefer. We don't like it, but it is a part of life we cannot avoid. There are conditions that can bring this about nearly anytime in life, but for most of us it will probable start to take place in our early seventies. Often between seventy-two and seventy-five.

Some of the stories you will read here will be written around these kinds of life's conditions. The thoughts expressed here may surprise many younger lovers, but not those who are in their later years. Some may seem far fetched, but they could happen. Pleasures of a sexual nature can be expressed in many manners so when you get older, keep an open mind. If you are an older person reading these stories, you may find a few ideas you had not considered before.

You no doubt, have heard the term. "Friends with Benefits." Of all the ages with a forgiving attitude this age group may be the one who could use these kinds of relationships the most. There are those who take advantage of this age group. That's a shame, but they will pay the price at some point themselves. Some of these stories are purely sexual. They are not written like erotic fiction, these get right down to the sexual content, and the bedroom language is blunt, but also commonly used. If you don't like this kind of language go no farther.

STORIES YOU WILL FIND HERE

Me & Thee - 1
Daily - 4
An Ideal Day - 5
Attractive, yes, or no. - 12
Benched - 16
Blind Sensitivity - 22
Bookends - 32
Competing - 37
Dan - 42
Dark of night - 53
Foursome - 71
Fred, Bill & Jackie - 74
Friends - 85
Frustrations - 90
Hands - 93
I'm not done yet - 95
I am, the way I am - 105
Lacy - 108
Love Symbols - 112
Marion - 115
Marti - 125
Muriel's Confession - 130
Nelli & Fred - 132
Odd - 143
Older - 146
Pants - 154
Posing - 158
Tables & Chairs - 164
The Baby Sitter - 166
The Butterfly - 177
The Dark of Night - 197

The Slut - 200
The Invitation - 207
The Office - 211
Two times Three - 214
Visiting - 227
Volunteer - 232
Watch - 235
Weekends - 238
Winter weather - 248
Lunch - 253

ME & THEE
I had been expecting John so when he knocked on my door I did not hesitate to open it, still I had the safety chain on, but after a quick peak I let him inside. With the door closed and locked behind him, he handed me a package. A gift, as it were. I knew what it was before I opened it. It is a very, very good woman's toy. Yes, a dildo. I understand this one will climax in a woman's vagina when she is ready for that to happen. A touch of reality I suppose. And, of course it will vibrate if that turns you on, and it does me.

John moved to a chair near my bed and began to take his shoes and socks off, but I moved in front of him and he hesitated. I was only wearing a Tee shirt and panties, so I said. "John, take my panties off."

He looked into my eyes and I could see the excitement in his eyes as he said. "Cheryl I'd like to take your panties off every day for the rest of our lives. In fact if it was possible I'd rather we were both bare assed most of the time."

As he reached up to take hold of the top of my panties and began to pull them down over my hips, I raised each leg higher than I normally would. I did this so he would see I was clean shaven for him. When he had them off, he said. "Turn around."

With my back to him he said. "Take off your Tee shirt and hand it to me. Then open your legs and lean over as far as you can without falling over."

As I leaned over and with my legs spread wide he began to rub the cheeks of my ass, and I liked that, but he was also looking at my pussy. I expected this from him because he is a pussy kind of lover. Also, his comments were a strong indication. Such as "Fuck. That's a beautiful pussy. God I want that." When he had enough of me at the moment, he said."Go sit on the bed while I finish getting undressed."

I sat on the edge of the bed, then leaned back and opened my legs so he could look between my legs, and I like that he does that. My tits are not as nice as they were when I was younger, but John doesn't care. As long as he can see them, Or that I can press them against him, or that he can get his hands or lips on, then he is eager to take me.

John stood up and took his shirt off, laid it down on the chair, then came to stand in front of me. He undid his belt, then the button at the top of his pants, then the zipper. He stepped out of them and put them with his shirt. Back in front of me he took off his shorts, and moved to put them with his pants. Now he was close to me and I began to explore him very closely.

He has a nice cock. It's average in length, but it is thicker than most men's cocks. When it is in you, you know you are full of him. I cupped his balls in one hand as I felt the length of him. My fingers tracing their way up and down its length. I pulled his foreskin back to reveal the ridge around the head of his cock. Knowing this would stop my lips from slipping off him. Either of my lips. High, or low. When I slipped my mouth over him, his hands came down on my head. Not to control me, but in affection for what I was doing to pleasure him

He waited several seconds before he said. "Cheryl. When you're satisfied with what you are doing, get your pussy up on the bed."

I let him go and moved up onto the bed, then moved kiddie corner across the bed when he told me how he wanted me. John moved up between my legs as his cock just lay between my legs and close to my pussy. He kissed me with a passion, then moved down to suck on my nipples. First one than the other. I was eager as I knew where he was going next. As he moved down between my legs, he gently rubbed the lips of my pussy, but not for long. When his mouth found my lips and his tongue worked its way inside to lick my clit, I knew it was going to be a wonderful climax.

DAILY

This is not something John actually does to me every day, but almost. As we spend a lot of our time wearing only Tee shirts around the house when we are alone, he will come up to me, whisper in my ear. "Cheryl, open your legs." And you know damn well I do as he asks. What he does is reach down between my legs and just briefly and gently, rubs my lips. He know this will make me hot and wanting him in me.

But I get even with him. Like yesterday. We were at the store and I came up behind him and said. "God, I'd like to suck your cock right now." He turned to me, kissed me and said. "You evil woman."

When we got home and were in the bedroom changing out of our street clothes he said. "Don't even bother getting dress yet. Get your ass on the bed."

I just grinned at him as I got ready for him. He fucked the hell out of me.

AN IDEAL DAY, AN IDEAL EVENING.
Lucy and I had been lucky when we came across
each other. We'd met at a friend's party and both
of us felt the other. As if our brains were talking to
each other before we'd spoken to each other. As if
our Aura's had mingled and understood the needs
we each felt. I'll spare you the first few times we
spent together, but we soon realized we might
never find anyone else who like to fuck as much as
we did.

Yesterday, Saturday, was not unusual for us. It was
an ideal day and an ideal evening. When I woke, a
little after eight in the morning, I'd gotten up and
went to the bathroom. When I came back to bed,
Lucy was laying on her right side facing my side of
the bed. Her arm was up on her hip and so when I
lifted the sheet up I could see her tits. Her left tit
was lying on top of the right one. I moved down in
the bed a bit, then moved over to Lucy so I could
suck on her nipples. Soon her hand came up to
hold my head, and she started to turn over on her
back. Slowly she turned and pulled me with her.
Of course now I was between her legs and her right
hand moved down to take hold of my hard cock.
She pulled me up, and after I let go of her nipple,
she guided me into her. We fucked long enough for
both of us to get off, then we got up and took our
showers.

We dressed in our usual indoor clothing, which is really just a long Tee shirts only. We dress this way so we are accessible to one another anytime.

It was late morning and I had been doing a couple of other things around the house. I happened to be heading toward the kitchen when I glanced into the living room. Lucy was watching a program she had tapped the day before, and her Tee shirt was pulled up to her waist. She was slouching way down on the couch so her pussy was on the edge of the seat and her fingers were rubbing her clit as she watched the show. She was in need and I was going to help her get through it anyway I could.

I got a drink, then went into the living room. I got a cushion from one of the corners of the couch and put it down on the floor between her legs. Then I got down on my knees and leaned over between her legs. She opened her legs wide for me and I started licking her pussy while she watched her show. I didn't let her get off, and I just kept her on the edge. When I moved out from between her legs, she said. "You're not stopping are you?"

"For the time I am. It looks like a nice day to be outside reading, don't you think?"

"That sounds nice. I'll be out in a few minutes, when my program is over."

"Okay. I'll get things ready."

I went out to the garage and got our two air Mattresses. I made sure they had enough air in them, then took them outside. I put them under our large Oak tree. The mattress nearest the tree would be Lucy's and the one nestled up against the bottom of hers, was mine. Back in the house I got a pillow for Lucy and a mystery novel for me. I was just getting comfy on my air mattress when Lucy joined me. She was carrying her Kindle book reader.

We do this often enough that we have a ritual in our heads already in place. Lucy laid down on the air mattress that was above my head. The one nearest to the tree. With her head on her pillow she arranged herself with her legs spread open and her knees raised. Then I settled my head between her legs and lay back on her mound. My arms were out under her knees, but I didn't open my book. Instead I just lay there enjoying the warmth of the afternoon breezes and the shaded sun keeping us warm.

"Are you going to read?" She asked me.

"Yeah. In a bit. I was just trying to remember what it was that Astrologer told us."

"You mean why we like to fuck so much?"

"Yeah. What was that? Do you remember?"

"Sure he said we have Venus in the first house, whatever that means. And when Venus is in that house it leads to addictions of some kind. Ours is in Capricorn, which for us happens to be sex. Any kind of sex."

We lay still for a bit and I knew Lucy had picked up her electronic book.

I had my eyes closed and was thinking how good Lucy is to fuck, when I felt her left hand come down on top of my forehead. Then she pulled me tighter against her. I said.
"Are you reading one of those fuck stories from that book, 'Bedtime Stories for Adults' again?"

"No. I finished that book. But, yes I am reading a fuck story only this one is in a book called, ' Pleasures of the Mind."

I pulled my arms in from under her legs, and raised up slightly between her legs to see her left hand now rubbing her nipples. I lowered my face down to lick her pussy. I like her reaction when I use my tongue on her. It makes her hotter than hell. After a bit she laid her Kindle down and both hands started rubbing and pulling at her nipples and her tits.

Then I could feel her raising slightly as if to take a cock into her pussy. When she started making her fuck noises, I pushed my tongue against her harder.

"Uh. . .uh. . .Oh fuck that's good. Oh God, just fuck me, Jimmy."

I raised up, wiped my mouth dry with the back of my hand, and moved up between her legs. As I moved up I guided my hardness into her wet. Then I fucked her with normal strokes. It only took a few minutes for her to get off. When I heard her Uh. . .Uh. . .Uh. . .then a long "Uummm." I jammed deep into her and felt her climax. When I fuck her out doors, she has intense climaxes.

I think all women have heavy climaxes when they get fucked outside. It's something about being out in the open and potentially exposed that leads to more excitement.

That evening I was watching a ball game, slouched back on the couch, and my legs open. Not for any particular reason, other than letting Lucy see my cock as she moved around the house. We do that. Exposing ourselves to each other, simply because we like seeing each others private parts. I like seeing her lean over so I can see her tits hanging down, or look between her legs to look at her pussy. She likes seeing my cock move around as I move around.

She was headed for the kitchen from our bedroom, and she stopped to ask me. "Can I get you anything?"

I heard her, but I only reached out to pat the couch next to me. I looked up just in time to see her smile before she went through the door into the kitchen. Moments later she was back and lay down on the other end of the couch. Her head resting on my tummy. Her hand holding my soft cock.

As I came up to attention, she moved down a bit and slid my cock into her mouth. Holding me there while I watched the game. Well fuck. You know how long that lasted. When I put my hand on top of her head, she got serious and began sucking me off. I pulled her hair back and off the side of her head so I could see her lips as she sucked on me. I came with a loud moan as I shot my cum into her. She milked me dry, then said. "You owe me a good fuck later."

"When you're ready, just come play with that cock."

When we went to bed that night, I lay on my back with Lucy cradled in the crook of my left arm. She had her tits pushed tight against me. When I felt her hand come down to stroke me with her fingers I knew she wanted to fuck. When my cock hardened, she rolled over onto her back and said.

"I'm ready."

I said. "You're always ready."

I moved over between her legs and opened her
with my fingers, then eased into her. I didn't rush
her, or myself. I just fucked her in our normal
strokes. As she came up to her peak, I stopped
pulling out and pushing into her. Instead I lay still,
but flexing my cock muscles inside of her. To her
it feels like it is pulsing with want and need of her.

"Oh fuck. Jimmy. I am almost there, I . . . Oh God
that feels good when you do that. Oh fuck I'm
gonna cum. Oh fuck, . . . oh fuck. . . Oohhh. . .
Uummm. . . . Aahhggg. . . . "

Then when she lay still, I fucked her for my own
fucking needs. I jammed into her loose body until I
fucking came. I pushed in deep and I let myself
flow.

ATTRACTIVE, YES, OR NO?

I'm not sure if attractiveness matters. I don't think of myself as a beautiful woman, nor gorgeous, or any of that. I may be attractive, but probably only to the men who are aware of women who are in need. Or, if you want to hear it said in a different manner, a woman who is in a constant state of being horny. I've been in a fairly solid relationship with a man for most of my life. Still, being contented with my sex life is not the same as being free of sexual needs. The man in my life does fuck me, but I could use someone with a lot more cock experience than he has. There is a solution to this condition, but it can cause problems if you are not very careful in your choosing. The condition is a 'Lover', or if you prefer, having a friend with benefits.

For instance, recently while I was speaking with a man I have known for years, and while we were at a family function and off to one side by ourselves for a few moments. I made up my mind to do something, so when our eyes met, in my mind I said. "Damn, why don't you fuck me."

As I implored him with my eyes, I think he read me, or at least caught on that I was telling him something. Later in the day I gave him a quick kiss goodby. Knowing that it was much to quick, but because there were others around that could see what was happening, I made it brief.

Then, at a later date, we were standing in my kitchen, he said. "Do you remember when our eyes met at the family gathering, and when you kissed me?"

MY heart skipped a beat, but I said. "Yes."

"Well, that kiss was much too short. So, I want to kiss you again."

I smiled and said. "Okay."

Instead of moving in to kiss me he said. "But first, I want you to see this." I watched as he reached down to pull down the zipper the pants he was wearing, he did this to open the fly on his pants.

I liked what he had done, but asked. "Why did you do that?"

"So that when I kiss you, if you feel the need, you can reach inside to hold me."

He reached up with both of his hands and took my head in them and kissed me quickly. Then he let go of me and said. "That's how our last kiss took place. But this is what I wanted it to be like."

His left hand came up behind my head and took hold of my hair. As he pulled my mouth to his I was already getting horny.

Our lips met, for only a moment, then they parted
and our tongues brought out a passion in both of
us, and my hand found its way inside his pants to
take hold of his cock.

He wasn't hard yet, but it didn't matter. I was
holding onto a good possible fun filled future. I
knew that any relationship with this man would be
safe.

When our mouths parted, he said. "Why don't you
go sit on your couch?"

I took his hand and led him to my living room
couch, and I sat down as he had asked. He moved
to one side and slipped his shoes off, then stood
right in front of me. He undid his belt, then the
button holding the top of his pants together, then
said. "Shall I stop, or go ahead?"

I did not hesitate. "Keep going."

He slid his pants and shorts down where he could
step put of them. He moved just far enough to put
them on the other end of the couch, then came
back in front of me. Then he took off his shirt
while I looked at him hanging down in front of my
face.

He tossed his shirt off toward his pants, then he started pulling at his cock. Picking it up and letting it drop. God, this was good, but when he reached out to take my hair in his hand again, and tugged me forward, I fucking near came. I slipped my mouth over the end of his cock and began sucking on him.

After a few moments he said. "Now, it's your turn." And he pulled his cock out of my mouth and sat on the couch beside me.

I took my shoes off and moved in front of him. I started with my Jeans and panties and after I had them off, and as his hands began to search all over me below the waist, I took off my blouse and bra. Oh fuck was I hot for him.

Then, I did like he had done to me. I reached out and pulled his head between my legs and I felt his tongue as it found its way to my clit.

I knew this was going to a lot of sexual fun in the future years to come.

BENCHED
A year ago, if someone had told me I'd do things like I do with Jon, I'd have said they were crazy. That I would never do these things. Well, when you meet a guy like Jon, a smooth talker, and a silver-tongued devil, you might consider doing exactly these kinds of things. It's not really dangerous things. It's more mentally daring. He just makes suggestions as to some kind of sexual event. The first time he did this I asked him, "Why would I do that?"

"Because you will like it."

Let me give you a couple of ideas of what I mean.

Like last week when I saw him walking toward me in the park where we had agreed to meet, and as he got near I saw him reach down inside his pants to adjust himself. I knew he did it so I could see him moving his cock around inside his pants. When he did this, I knew he was as horny as I was. We both knew what was going to take place as he settled in next to me on the picnic bench. Well, at least I had an idea of what was going to happen.

He'd asked me to meet him here at this picnic table, and as he came up next to me, he leaned over to kiss me. When he did this, I felt his hand start at my shoulder, then slip slowly down my back, ultimately to my butt.

It was if he was caressing me, but in reality I knew he was feeling me to see if I was wearing a bra and panties, because he had asked me not to. I wasn't.

He sat down next to me with his back leaning against the top of the picnic table. My arms were resting on the table top. He was facing one direction, I the other, and opposite direction. The words we spoke were just about stuff we didn't really care about, but as we begin to talk his hand reached down for the hem of my dress and he lifted it up above my knees. His hand was cold as he reached up under my dress and I really didn't care. I opened my legs so he could reach what he treasured between my legs. The very spot he desired to tease. The very spot that he knew would make me cum. As a noisy fuck, I had to stifle my cries of pleasure when I came. I mean we were at a public park with people wandering all about. A woman screaming would have drawn immediate attention. Even a scream of pleasure as she is driven over the top of sexual pleasure sitting on a picnic bench.

After I had cum two times, Jon pulled his hand out from under my dress, then, on a tissue, he dried the wetness on his hand that had come from my pussy. Before we left the park, he said. "You should go out onto your deck and sit in one of your chairs and masturbate."

"Jon. I can't do that. There are people who wander around the area."

"Yes, you can. You can drape a large towel, or something over the deck railing to keep you out of view, unless it is after dark. Then don't use anything, just go out and sit in the dark, but take a toy and get off. More than once, if you can."

I thought about this the rest of the day, and even though I had a strong tendency not to do the very thing he had suggested, and I cleaned my deck chairs off. Jon wasn't going to be here, but he knew I'd tell him about it if I did it. So, late afternoon, I draped a towel over the railing, got myself a glass of wine, a fuck book I've been reading, my toy, and took them out to the small table next to my chosen deck chair.

In my bedroom I got undressed, then walked naked down to the sliding door leading out to my deck, and looked around. I couldn't see anyone at the moment so I quickly slipped out and sat in the deck chair. It felt good right away. Being naked outside was .. . . nice. Sexually daring, and I was getting wet just sitting here naked.

I reached for my toy and slipped it into my wetness, then I picked up my glass of wine. I sipped some wine, then after setting the glass back on the table, I picked up the book of short sexual fiction I had been reading. As I started reading a new story, and as it made me even more horny, I started moving my toy in and out of my pussy.

I came twice before I even finished the story. I think a lot of the pleasure came from just being out here and doing this to myself. Though the story helped, as did the thinking about Jon.

I called Jon afterwards and told him what I'd done. Then he told me to be outside at ten o'clock, which would be after it got dark. I was to wait for him and to sit naked on my deck chair until he got here. At ten, I was nude, and turned off my lights, then I went out to sit on the deck chair. I was barely settled when I heard someone. "Jon, is that you?"

"Yes. You will be able to see me slightly after your eyes get used to the dark. Tell me when you can see me okay."

I heard him coming up the steps to my deck, and could finally see him. "I can see you now."

"Okay. Come to me and take my hand."

He was standing on the top step, and as I took his hand in mine, he said. "Come with me."

"Where are we going?"

"We are going to walk down to the pond, then back. And on the way back I'll tell you what I'd like you to do next."

"Jon, I'm naked."

"I know. Come with me."

I figured everyone else was home, and probably in bed by now. So, I took his hand and he led me down the path to the pond. It felt wonderful to be naked out here like this. And I wanted to fuck right on the edge of the pond, but I knew that wasn't what he had planned for me. On the way back to my place, he told me in detail what he wanted next.

After I was inside my living room, I could hear Jon closing the sliding door behind us. Then I could hear him following me up the steps to my bedroom. As he got undressed, I put two pillows on the bed and got on my hands and knees. I waited for him to get to me, knowing that when he was ready I was to lie down over the pillows. The pillows were going to be right under my hips and would raise my ass into the air a bit. When Jon was undressed, I felt him getting on the bed behind me, then he moved between my spread legs. As his left hand was on my left hip, he guided his cock into my pussy.

After he was inside me, he leaned over and put his full weight on my back. As he lay on me, his hands found their way under my tits, then he said. "Lay down now."

I stretched my arms out in front of me, and as the rest of my body came down onto the bed, his hands were trapped under my tits. Then he started fucking me. Every time he came down on me, the cheeks of my ass bounced, and my pussy was filled with his cock. Each time I came, I told him I was cumming, but he kept fucking me. Finally his strokes came faster and faster, and he was telling me things like. "God that's a good cunt. Fuck you feel good," then, as he hammered me deeply, he said. "I'm gonna fill you full now. Right fucking noowww."

As we were both washing ourselves in my bathroom, I happen to look into the mirror. I could see his hand prints all over both of my tits.

"You wanna know what we are gonna do next time?"

"No, what?'

"I'm gonna fuck you outside."

BLIND SENSITIVITY

I'd been to the 'Women's Wish' group some years
ago. I have to admit it was a very enjoyable
experience and I remember many of the details
vividly. Once you have been invited to join the
club, you can opt to receive their newsletter.
Which is not sent often enough in my mind.
However, I want to tell you about the one I found
in my e-mail a week or so ago. It offered an
experience that I'd not heard of before and it was
labeled. "Blind Sensitivity" I wondered about it for
a bit, but out of curiosity I sent my previous
account number and a question to them. I had
asked what it was all about? The reply did little to
explain it in any detail. It simply read.

*"Marie. This offer is limited to a few members
only. It is designed to put you in touch with your
own sensitivities. To experience your feelings in
more depth than you would normally feel."*

During the night I thought about the note. I'm
older now than the first time I went to see them.
And, I'm alone at this point in my life. I have
friends but no one I'm going to bed with at the
time. I got up about three this morning and sent a
request to accept their offer. I had an answer before
noon.

"Your appointment is for one O'clock tomorrow afternoon. A car was will arrive for you about twelve thirty, the driver will deliver you to our present location, and return you to your residence when you are ready. We suggest you wear loose clothing."

I was very ever ready when the long black limousine arrived at exactly twelve thirty. A young guy came to my door and knocked softly. When I opened it, he smiled and said.

"I am your driver. When you are ready, we can leave."

"I am ready."

He stood to one side and motioned me forward. I locked my door, then moved out to the car. The driver opened the rear door for me, then closed it when I was seated. The windows were tinted to a dark color, though I could see out, no one could see inside where I was sitting.

We arrived in a warehouse area which surprised me, and he drove up to one of the large buildings. As we approached the building, a large metal door rolled up to allow the car to drive inside. Inside the building it was different than you might have expected. It was not a dinghy old building at all. Instead it was brightly lit and painted in soft colors.

The driver opened my door and offered me his hand. Another man was waiting and he led me to an ornately carved door, opened it and I entered the plush office area.

A Young woman was seated behind a desk. She was dressed very provocatively. She quickly glanced down at a desk notepad, then looked up at me and said. "Ah. Marie."

I looked at her and said. "Yes."

"Please, you can go into the waiting room. It will only be a few minutes wait."

She buzzed another door open for me, and I was led into another inner office. Before she left me, she said. "Please. Make yourself comfortable. You can glance through our staff brochures while you are waiting."

I sat on a very comfortable couch and picked up a leather bound book from the top of a coffee table. God, the men it displayed looked damn good. Most of them much too young for me, but it stirred me anyway. They were all nude of course, and with a few close ups of each of them.

Of course the close up photos were mostly of their penis's. Sizes ranged from five or so inches, some were so long I doubt many women could even begin to take them inside.

It was only moments before a different woman came for me. She led me to a changing room and before she left she handed me a white sleeping mask. "You will need to wear this so that you cannot see what is going on."

"I am not to see what is going to happen?"

"No. Your session is to experience your own sensitivities. You cannot do this if you can see normally. You must be blind, in a sense, to fully enjoy this session. When you are ready put your mask on and someone will come for you."

"Should I get undressed?"

"No. Your companion will take care of that. Also, you can speak to him, but any conversation with him will be sexual."

I put the mask on as soon as she left the room and it was only a moment before I heard the door open. A warm hand found mine as he said. "Come with me, Marie." And he tugged at me indicating I was to follow him. I felt odd not seeing where we were going, but he took care that I did not bump into anything. We did not go far and when we stopped he let go of my hand, He then I felt his hands as he began to unbutton my dress. I felt his fingers as he undid each button. I could feel him lifting the hem of my dress up and then he pulled the dress up over my head.

He reached down to remove my shoes, then his thumbs then hooked inside the waistband of my panties and he pulled them down over my hips and down so I could step out of them.

"Ahh, you are indeed a beautiful woman." It excited me to know he could see my ass and my pussy, especially because I keep my pubic hair cut very short.

Next He was behind me and undoing my bra. With the hooks open, his chest touched my back as he pulled it over my shoulders and down my arms. Then I felt his presence as he came back around in front of me. His hands rested on my shoulders as he pushed lightly so as to make me move backwards.

"Please sit down, Marie."

I came in contact with something behind me, then he put his hands under my elbows and lifted me slightly. I knew he wanted me to sit on the thing behind me, and as I put my hands out to my sides to lift myself, I could feel something on each side of me. Instinctively I felt each of them and asked.

"Are these stirrups like in my doctor's office?"

"Yes. They will support your feet while I am enjoying myself between your legs."

When I was up on the cushion, I could feel a soft back to the seat I was sitting on. Like a nice comfortable office chair. He raised each of my feet, one at a time and placed them in a cupped place on each of the stirrups. I knew I was sitting with my legs spread open. I was exited about what he'd said.

"And how are you going to enjoy yourself between my legs?"

"I'm going to start by kissing you inside your inner thighs. It is nice that you have fleshy pussy lips because I can tease them with my tongue. But first, are your nipples sensitive?"

"Not unless you bite them."

"Do you like a man to have his hands on your tits and playing with your pussy?"

Fuck. I was already hot and now he's asking me this. "God, yes. I love a man to explore me with his hands, and with his tongue."

"So. You enjoy oral sex?"

"Yes, and I'm so wet now, you'll probably need a towel."

"I want you to pay attention to things I'm doing to you. You will find your senses become much more attuned to your physical body than you have probably experienced before."

I sensed him moving between my legs, then when his lips touched me between the thighs I felt a shudder go through my entire body. He kissed me up the inside of one upper thigh, then moved over to the other side. When his tongue licked the lips of my pussy, my hands clenched and my feet tightened. As he tried to force me open with his tongue, my whole body tried to scoot down to meet him. "Oh my God, that feels good."

He worked my clit until I was on the verge of climaxing, then he stopped licking my pussy. He came closer and his mouth was now sucking on my nipples. I could also feel the tip of his cock rubbing against the lips of my pussy. I raised my hands to pull his face tighter to my tits, and when I did, he started to push his cock into me. Believe me I tried to scoot down so he could get into me, but I couldn't move down any farther. This guy was magic in the way he teased my fucking pussy.

But then I began to feel every inch of him slipping slowly into me. When he was all the way in, he gave me quick thrust to bump me deep inside. I fucking climaxed, and I knew damn well I needed more.

"Oh, God. Take me off of this chair thing and fuck me good."

He reached his hands behind me, and pulled me to him. "Put your arms around my neck and your legs around my waist."

When I did as he said. He lifted me from the seat and began to walk holding me impaled on his cock. We ended up on a bed and then he started to fuck me good. He hammered into me until I fucking came again. Then he slow fucked me until I did it again.

After a bit he said. "I'm going to fuck you now, but not for you. I'm going to fuck you for myself."

"Oh, yes, yes, yes."

"After that we will lay and rest a bit. Then I want you to suck my cock and then I want you to get on top of me and fuck me until you cum again."

When I started sucking his cock I was surprised. Not because I was holding a man's cock in my mouth, I've done this many times. But the feeling of it as I moved my mouth up and down on it let me pay more attention to how it is shaped.

When you can just look at a man's cock it is easy to see the details. When you can't see it, you have to feel the parts of it.

Sucking him made me want to feel him in my pussy because it would almost feel like his cock was still in my mouth. I moved up over him and sat down on his hard shaft. As I eased down onto him, I paid more attention to the feeling of being penetrated. It made me want him deep inside me and not in a few minutes. I wanted him in me and right fucking now. Then I slammed myself down on his cock. Being in control of how you are being fucked gives it a higher intensity. I think. It was only a minute or se before I came again.

The woman from the second office, finally came to me and said. "Marie. I'm sorry but there are others waiting for Todd."

BOOKENDS

I have two men in my life. Okay, I have two men in life who fuck me. In a sense I think for the way I like things, I have the ultimate arrangement. One young guy, and one old guy. The young guy, Ron, is kinda rough with me. He uses me more for his needs than mine. It's like I'm his bitch to fuck when he wants to. He possesses me. He fucks me hard, and often fast as well. It's like he hammers my climaxes to the surface. His hard thrusts beat against my clit, and each stroke jacks me up one more notch. And when I cum it's most often intense and leaves me drained. Let me give you a basic idea of things he does.

A few days ago we were standing at a highway overlook checking out the view before us. He made me take off my panties while we stood there then lean over the rock wall so he could fuck me from behind. The damn rocks were hard, but so was he, and I got rammed good. Or, if we are at my place he will say things like. "Lets go fuck." I mean, in a sense he is crude, though he doesn't mistreat me. You know, abusively. I have no fear of him. He has a few very soft pieces of rope that he uses to tie my hands and feet to the corners of the bed, you know, spread eagled, then he fucks me that way. This kind of stuff may scare some of you, but if you know the guy, and trust him, it can be kinda fun. And sometimes I like the roughness of how he fucks me.

However, then there is Leonard.

Leonard, the older guy is older. Much older. And I don't care, you see he has years of experience and has taken the time to learn what I like done to me. He also knows he can make me submissive to him. He knows I like to be that way, but Ron doesn't know this because he hasn't taken the time to learn this about me. The first time Len made me submissive to him was while we were driving around, Leonard told me. "Get undressed."

And if I asked. "Now?"

"Of course now."

So, I got undressed while we were driving down the road in the car. He said he wanted to be able to reach over to touch me when he wanted to. I think he did it more so I would feel exposed to anyone who might happen to look into his car as we were driving around. It made me horny to be this way and he knew that's what would happen. He also asks me questions, which if I answer incorrectly, will get me spanked. Such as. "Are you horny?" If I say. "Yes' He will smack her on the ass for the one word answer. What he wants is something like. "Fuck yes, I'm horny." You know, bedroom language.

The last time he came to see me, and when I opened the door for him he just stood outside my apartment door looking in at me, then said. "Get undressed."

"Right now. Standing in my doorway?"

"Yes. Right now."

I hesitated, but not for long. After I had my clothes off, he said. "Come out here and kiss me."

"Oh, Jeez, Len."

"Come to me."

I leaned out to look up and down the hallway. It was quiet and no one was around. So I rushed out and kissed him passionately. As our lips parted, he said. "Now, walk down the hall a ways, and then come back to me."

Fuck I was nervous. I walked down the hall about ten feet or so, then walked back. But it excited me much more than I expected. He was watching me walk, and looking to see how my tits moved as I walked. Now I was really ready for his cock, and I wanted it anyway I could get it. I ducked into my apartment, and he followed me inside. After the door was closed, and locked.

He took hold of my left nipple and pulled me to
my bedroom. Fuck, if you like your nipples
pinched, or some nipple pain, get a man to lead
you around by your nipples like a pull toy.

In my bedroom he had me lay down on the edge of
my bed while he got undressed. He sat on a chair
to take off his shoes and socks, then he came to
stand in front of me. As he pulled his pants and
shorts off, he stood for a moment with his cock
hanging just inches from my face, then he moved
back to the chair to leave his clothes there and took
his shirt of at the same time.

When he came back to me he reached down and
took one of my nipples in his fingers, pinched it
hard and pulled me to him. I knew what he wanted
me to do, and he knew I would do as he wanted.
So, submissive as I am, I leaned over and took him
in my mouth. I knew he would tell me what he
wanted me to do next while I was sucking his
cock.

"I want you to lay right there on top of your bed.
I'm going to open the curtains on your windows."

I pulled off his cock and said. "Len. I told you
about the teenage kids who live next door to me.
Both the boy and the girl have upstairs bedrooms
and I have seen them peeking over at me when the
curtains are open."

"I know. Sexual education has to start sometime."
He opened the curtains and then he came over to
me. "Open your legs for me."

I spread my legs, and watched him move onto the
end of the bed. He moved up over me and I could
feel the head of his cock dragging on my mound. I
reached down and guided him into me as he
lowered himself down on top of me. As he started
to fuck me, I glanced quickly out the window, and
I'm sure I saw some kind of movement at one of
the windows of the house next door. I thought,
"Fuck it." Then I paid attention to what Leonard
was doing to me.

He likes me to tell him when I'm cumming. And it
didn't take long before I told him. "Len. I'm going
to cum. Now, Len. Right fucking nowww. . . .Oh
God that's good. Oh fuck don't stop, Len, make
me cum again."

Sometimes we will watch a porno film on
television together and when we do it isn't unusual
for Leonard to stroke his cock. I like to watch him
when he does this, but most of the time I will just
move up over him and sit on his cock facing him
and fuck him. He will hold my tits in his hands
with my nipples between his fingers. He gets off
quickly this way. Being fucked and watching
others fuck on television really works on his
voyeuristic mind.

Leonard uses my kinky needs, Ron doesn't even
know about them. I don't tell him because I don't
think he would know how to do this stuff. I'm sure
he wouldn't lick my clit, but Leonard does it just
fine. Fuck, it makes me hot thinking about that.

FOURSOME

Okay. I'll have to give you some background info
before I tell you how today went. You see a few
years ago I came across a guy, Larry, who ended
up being a friend with benefits. So when I was
horny I could get in touch with Larry and he would
come take care of my needs. However, in recent
months I met a new fella, Tom. Whom I'm getting
serious about, and when I told Larry I had a new
love life and that I couldn't play sexual games with
him anymore, he seemed to understand the
situation. Then, last week he sent me a note saying
how much he missed me. Poor guy, he just needed
someone to fuck and I wasn't available to him
anymore.

Then I had an idea. I sent my sister an e-mail and
told her about Larry and asked her opinion.
Actually I was asking her more than that, but
didn't have to come right out and say what I
wanted. She understood. She had agreed to come
over today if Larry was going to be here. After she
had given me her answer, I sent a note to Larry
asking him if he could come by today, and he had
said. "Damn right."

So, my new love life, Tom was sitting by me on
one couch, my sister, Chrissy, was sitting on
another couch across from us, and we were waiting
for Larry to show up. Well, we weren't exactly
waiting because Tom was sitting next to me and he

didn't have any pants on and I was playing with his cock while Chrissy watched. I only had a loose dress on so he could reach between my legs when he wanted too. This stuff going on had stirred Chrissy so much she had gone into my bedroom and taken off her panties and bra, then came back to sit across from us with her legs spread open so Tom could see up her dress. She likes men like I do.

When I heard the knock at the door I got up and motioned for Chrissy to come with me. We opened the door to find Larry standing there. He looked at the two of us, then he stepped inside. With the door closed, I kissed him, deeply and wantingly. Then I stepped back and said. "This is my sister, Chrissy. I think you met her once a year or so ago?"

"Yes. I do remember."

I watched his eyes exploring Chrissy because the top buttons of her dress were undone and he could see her breasts. Quite easily, I might add. Then she took the initiative, and said. "Are you going to kiss me hello as well?"

Larry moved over to her, put his hand up behind her head and pulled her mouth to his. When their lips met I could see the hunger in both of them growing, so I went back to sit by Tom, and waited.

When they came up for air, Chrissy took his hand and led him to the couch across from us, but before he sat down, she tugged at his pants and said.

"You might as well take these off. If you don't, you'll only be uncomfortable and wish you had."

Larry took his shoes off, then stood in front Chrissy. Facing her he opened his belt, then undid the top button to his pants. After he unzipped them, he pulled his pants and his shorts down over his hips and stepped out of them. He stood there a moment in front of her and tugged at his cock, tempting it to become harder than it already was. Chrissy patted the couch next to her indicating he should sit there on her right side. Which he did. Nothing was said for a few long seconds as the four of us watched and as Chrissy and I were holding a man's cock in our hands, feeling the hardness and wanting it inside of us. Anywhere inside of us.

I moved over slightly, bent over and lowered my mouth down over Tom's cock and began to suck on him. Out of the corner of my eye, I saw Chrissy doing the same to Larry's cock. What a sight that must have been. Two women sucking cock in the same living room and at the same time.

It wasn't long before I heard Larry say. "Chrissy, lets go fuck."

I was still sucking on Tom, but I saw them get up and go into my bedroom. I stopped sucking on Tom and we listened to them in the bedroom. We could hear Chrissy as Larry came down on her with each stroke. "Uhh. . . Uhh. . . Uhh. . .Uhh."

Tom got up and tugged at my hand. "Lets go join them."

I followed behind him and when we got into the bedroom, and we saw them fucking off to one side of my King size bed so there was room for us to fuck on the bed next to them.

I got up on the bed and opened my legs for Tom. He mounted me and we started to fuck. I had my head turned toward Chrissy and Larry. As I watched them fucking it made me hotter because I knew what was happening to Chrissy. As I listened to the slurping noises coming from them and I figured she must be a very wet fuck. That combined with Larry's long cock was what was making the slurping noises each time he pulled out and pushed back into her pussy on each stroke. She probably has never had a cock like Larry's, because he has a nice long dong.

When Chrissy came, the whole bed shook with her sexual convulsions. 'She didn't scream or anything like that, but it was a deep and prolonged moan of pleasure that came from her lips.

Just hearing her brought me to a climax. Tom hadn't made it yet so he kept fucking me while they watched us.

Just before Tom shot his cum in me, I heard Chrissy say. "Larry do you eat pussy?"

"Damn right."

"What say we go to my place, take a shower, and then you get me off using your tongue and I'll suck you off. Then we can get a bite to eat."

"I like that idea. Then after we've had something to eat, we can do some serious fucking."

As they walked out my front door, I was thinking. "Chrissy won't be able to walk comfortably tomorrow. Because when Larry says, he wants to get a serious fuck in. It will last for hours. She'll get used to his length, but it may take awhile before she's ready for a serious fuck with Larry. She'll call me. I know she will.

She'll complain about what I've unleashed on her, and all the while there will be a huge smile on her face. She'll probably be rubbing her clit while she's talking to me.

COMPETING

I was having coffee with Marilyn, my neighbor from across the street and friend for a number of years. We were in her kitchen at the table and she said. "I was behind two of your cousins in the store yesterday. They were talking quietly, but I heard them say something about going to the 'Cockfights.' I didn't know they still had those kinds of things. I thought they were ruled illegal years ago?"

I had to smile, then said. "You're talking about the fights between chickens."

"Well, yes."

"My cousins were talking about an event that happens every couple of years in our family."

"You have cockfights"

I almost laughed. "No. The men in our family have a contest."

"I don't understand?"

"Okay. I'll explain it to you, but you cannot ever tell anyone else about this. Every other year we get together and we rent the Lake view Hotel. We use the entire building for one night.

42

The owners put up a 'No Vacancy' sign and retire to their apartment leaving us with complete run of the place.

There are twenty-four rooms and we use almost all of them depending on how many women from the family show up and how many volunteers we get.

What happens at first is that the women choose a room, then hang out the "Do Not Disturb sign," and then they get undressed and wear only a robe tied with a cloth belt. When they are ready, they all meet in the large conference room. No one knows which room which woman is in. The men come in and choose one of the large chairs in the conference room, which are by now numbered. My grandfather usually takes chair number one, my father takes chair number two, then my brothers-in-law take chairs three, four and five. This year my oldest son will get chair number six. And we Have a guest spot for another man from outside the family who will be in number seven.

The men will get undressed when our scorekeeper, an independent outsider, tells them too. She doesn't participate and only keeps score. The men sit naked in their chairs, with their legs apart so the women can see how they look, and I mean how they look between the legs. The scorekeeper stands behind the men watches each man's cock to see who gets hard first, then second, and so on. She

43

records this as it happens. Then the women parade down the row in front of the men. As they do, they can show any part of themselves they want to, but they cannot touch the men.

Each woman is given points for each cock that gets hard as the men look at her. As each man gets a hard on, then Marjory measures their length and that is also recorded.

"God, it sounds complicated?"

"It really isn't. The last part of the contest is to see how long the men can last fucking a woman. They have to wait ten minutes after all of the women have left the conference room, then they take their cell phone with my phone number set up on it as a speed dial number with them, and they go out into the hall and choose any room they want. They give the woman in that room the phone and as soon as the man reaches his climax, the woman dials the number and his number is recorded by the scorekeeper. She has my phone. The man who lasts the longest wins that part of the contest. He, and the woman he is with, will get one point for each twenty minutes he fucks her without cumming."

"Oh my. Well, Beverly I'm curious. You said you were going to be a part of this. What happens if your son should choose your room?"

"I'd merely tell him he has to go choose a different room. I'd do the same thing if my husband chose my room. That way both of them would think I was just going to watch television until we were all called back to the conference room. Until all of the men are back in the conference room, the women stay in their rooms.

When all of the men have returned, Marjory calls each room, and the women wait ten minutes before they come back and join the others in the conference room."

"Do you have room for one more volunteer?"

"Yes. Does this mean you want to be with us?"

"Damn right."

"Okay, but you should know that the odds of your getting fucked are only one in four or, so."

"Still, it sounds like fun."

"Okay. Meet us at the Hotel at seven O'clock Friday night. I suggest you dress in loose clothing."

*   *

I was waiting in the lobby for Marilyn when she showed came and I said. "Pick any room that

45

doesn't have a 'Do Not Disturb' sign out on the doorknob then when you're ready meet us in the conference room down at the end of this hall."

When she came into the conference room, she came over to where I was sitting and pulled out the chair next to me as she said. "God I am so fucking horny. I've been thinking about this ever since you told me about it."

*   *

When Marjory, our scorekeeper, was satisfied, she said. "Okay, gentlemen you can get undressed, and sit in your chair."

I couldn't help but watch the women looking at the men while they got undressed. They were looking at the men's cocks. A few hands disappeared under the tables, we were all sitting at, and I had no doubt rubbing a tender place between their legs. When the men were all seated and their legs spread open, the scorekeeper moved over behind them so she could watch to see who got hard and when. Then she went down the list she had and called each woman to start their stroll down the line of men. She went over the rules with them telling them that they could do anything they wanted, but they could not touch the men.

46

It seemed to drag on forever, but most women didn't use the five minutes they were given to excite the men. Most of them would just walk down in front of the men, pull her robe open so they could see them naked. My son, Richard, got a hard on with every woman who let him see her. I knew he was way too excited to last long.

As it happened, Marilyn went just before it was my turn and she was a lesson to the rest of us. She walked to the center of the group of men, and pulled her robe off, dropping it on the floor. Then she leaned over and put her hands on her knees.

It was when she wiggled her hanging tits at them that many cocks came up hard. I could see her smile as she turned around. With her back to the men, she spread her legs wide apart and bent over so far she could almost touch her toes. Every cock sprang up to a full erection as each man was looking at a cleanly shaved pussy from between her legs. After she wiggled her ass at them, she picked up her robe and came back to the chair next to me. I knew I didn't have a chance in hell of competing with that kind of show.

I took my robe off before I left my chair and let them watch me as I walked and moved around in front of them. My tits bouncing and swaying back and forth as I moved. My son stared at me. He was looking at his mother naked for the first time. Still, he got a hard on, which I actually enjoyed. I turned around so they could see my ass, then I came back to my seat.

Marjory sent us to our rooms to wait. If we were one of those chosen, we had to be fair and make the call as soon as a man climaxed while he fucked us. I got into my bed but left the covers up over me stopping just below my tits. This kept a chill off, but left me open for their eyes to see, and I have nice tits for a woman my age.

My door opened and when I saw who it was I was surprised. So was he. He said. "I'm sorry hon., I can go choose a different room."

"Yes, you could."

"I have to tell you though. I've always wanted to fuck you."

This caught me off guard. "You have?"

"Always."

I thought about it for a few seconds too long, then said. And as I saw his cock getting hard, I "What the hell. You're here, come to bed."

When he was in bed with me he leaned over and kissed me gently, but that kiss invited another one, and that one started the fires burning. He moved down in the bed and put his lips on each of my tits in turn, sucking at my nipples one at a time. Fuck, this man was sucking my fuck juices right up to my pussies brim. His hand was between my legs and when he felt my wetness, he moved between my legs and they gave way to his needs. He opened me with his fingers and guided his hard cock into my wet waiting pussy. He didn't fuck me hard and fast. We both knew he had to last as long as he could. I have to tell you I wasn't minding the slow fuck. When a man can give you the feeling he is swinging his cock around inside your pussy and it is rubbing you on one side, then the other, you don't rush him. Even after I climaxed the second time, he kept fucking me. My pussy was so excited and sensitive from each previous climax that the following ones came easily.

*   *

The next morning my phone rang and I knew who it was without question. I picked it up and said. "Yes the coffee is done. Come on over."

When Marilyn came in my back door, she made herself at home. She poured herself some coffee, then refilled my cup. She was all smiles as she sat down. Looking at me, she said. "So, who won?"

"Only the contest winners know."

"So I didn't win anything?"

"Are you kidding me? You were almost last, except for the hard cock contest. Of course when you only have one point in the length of a fuck column, it doesn't help"

"Yeah. I know. He came almost as soon as he pushed into me. Of course I can't tell you who it was."

"He's young yet. He'll get better."

"Your son is hung."

"Yeah. I think he stirred every woman in the room."

"After I made the call, he stayed and fucked me two more times."

"Did he?"

"Yeah. When he opened my door, he said. "Oh, Hi." Then he smiled and asked if he could come in. I just wiggled my fingers at him. He didn't waste any time with me. But, when I looked at him I didn't need any time. He climbed on top of me, and I reached down to open myself. God, I had to tell him. "Wait. Fuck, go easy. Let me adjust to you."

"So, how did it go after that?"

"Well, after I made the required call to Marjory, he fucked me again. This time I could take his length, but the third time he fucked me was the best."

"Is he going to want to see you again?"

"I don't know, but it wouldn't surprise me. I'll cross that bridge when I get to it." It was quiet for a few moments while we sipped our coffee, then she said. "Did you have a good time?"

"I had a very good fuck, if that's what you mean."

"Did your inlaw's have a good time?"

"So they told me."

"How about your husband?"

"I don't know. We never talk about this afterwards."

"How about the old man?"

"I don't think he chose anyone. I think he stayed in a vacant room, then just called in after a reasonable time."

"How about your dad?"

"He had a damn good time."

"How about. . . . ."

"Marilyn. Enough with the questions.

"Can I come to the next one?"

DAN

Yesterday, Dan had called me when he was about a half hour away from my house. Dan was bringing things to me from my deceased grandmothers home. It was about a six hour trip for him to deliver this stuff to me, and I was appreciative. I was dressed when he backed the small rental furniture van up into my driveway. I say dressed, because I am not usually really dressed this time of day. I work at home, but I also work nights. Quite often at the end of my work day, my motherhood day begins. I get my two boys up, fix them breakfast and their school lunch, and send them on their way to school. After they are gone, I go to bed and sleep until around two or so in the afternoon, and get up to greet them when they get home from school. It works well for all of us.

Yesterday, however, my normal routine was dramatically altered. Dan, who lived across the street from my grandmother, had just gotten out of the navy and had volunteered to bring my stuff to me. I helped him getting my stuff in the house, still, it took us a couple of hours to get it inside and in places where I wanted it to go, at least for the time being. When we were done, I looked at Dan and he seemed to very warm. "Dan, you okay?"

"Yeah, just hot and sweaty."

"I can fix you an iced tea?"

"That would be good."

As I was fixing his tea, he was sitting at my kitchen table, in a chair that was facing me at my kitchen counters, and I asked. "Anything else?"

"Well, I need to cool off, then a shower would be good."

"Okay. The shower my boys use is probably a mess because I haven't been in there yet to clean it up, but you can use the one off my bedroom. I'll get you some fresh towels and bring them into you."

"Okay, but I have to cool off first. If I take a shower too soon, I'll just start to sweat again after the shower."

"Okay. Not that it matters, but how long does it take you to cool off?"

"It's quicker if I can take some clothes off." He said this with a smile on his face, and I was soon to understand why.

"Well, do what you have to do to get cool. Then you can take a shower."

"Before I started over here, I thought I understood you to say that I could use your spare bedroom to sleep in tonight?"

"Yes. It down the hall and the last door on the right."

He got up and walked down the hallway. When he came back, he sat in the same chair and as I started walking toward him with his iced tea, and with one in my other hand for myself, I saw he was only wearing boxer shorts. I could not help but look down, and I wasn't sure if he had arranged himself for me, of if it was natural, but, I could see the end of his prick peeking out from under the edge of his shorts. I could also see the swelling of him leading down to the head of his prick. I went around to the other side of the table so I couldn't see that part of him. Though, I must admit it did stir me.

As we talked sitting there, he asked. "I understand you work for the justice department?"

I laughed. "Well, not quite. I go to the courthouse late afternoons to pick up the court clerk's daily transcriptions from trials. Then I bring them home and spend the night writing them up on a word processor. Then I make two printed copies as well. The next afternoon I return the original transcript with my two printed copies, and I pick up that days records, and start all over again."

He looked deep in thought, then said."That's kinda
of a neat job."

"Yes. It is. And they pay me quite well, too."

"So, you have to work tonight then?"

"No. Actually I'm off this week. There are not
court cases being tried this week."

I think we sat there about a half an hour, when he
said. "I'm ready for that shower now."

I led him down to my bedroom and showed him
my large shower. It is one of those big glass wall
showers. It was in the house when I bought it, and I
like it. I said. "You can take your shower whenever
you like and I'll go get you some fresh towels."

When I had come back, Dan was in the shower. I
didn't even think about it, I just hung a large towel
up and over one end of the shower wall so he could
get it easily. I looked at him in the shower and he
made it a point to soap his prick and balls up while
I looked at him. Then I sat down on top of the
toilet lid. He pulled his hand down his shaft and it
seemed to take a long time to get to the end. He
was hard now, excited from my being close and
watching him. He started to just make slow strokes
of his prick, and each time he would go back up to
the base of his prick, it would leave the end caked

with a bulb of soapy foam. It looked like a large golf ball. I had no way of knowing, but he looked to be about eight or nine inches long, and big around as well. I spoke without thinking. "God, Dan. You're well endowed."

He looked up at me and said. "What?"

"Nothing, Dan. I'll go fix another iced tea." I just had to get out of there. Horney is the word that comes to mind, and I haven't been this way in some time. Probably because my life is too odd to spend much time with men.

As I walked down the hall toward my kitchen, I thought. The word other women use in reference to someone like Dan, is probably, "Hung."

When Dan found me in the kitchen, he stood by me at the stove and asked. "Any thing I can do to help you?"

"No. I'm just getting stuff ready for dinner. We eat early around here so the boys and I have some time together in the evenings."

He looked at the clock on the wall and said. "Man, today just disappeared. It's later than I thought."

He had just finished talking when the front door opened and Tony and Jimmy came inside. Then two boys came to the table and put their books down on top. Tony, my oldest said. "You must be, Dan? Mom said you were bringing a bunch of stuff to us from Grandma's house?"

"I am, and I did."

"I'm Tony and this is my brother, Jimmy."

The boys settled in after they put their jackets and stuff away, then they sat at the table to do their homework. I watched as the three of them sat at the table. Dan was reading my morning newspaper and the boys were mumbling about one thing and another. Suddenly Dan got up and with the newspaper in his hand he went to the bedroom and I could hear him talking on his cell phone.

By the time he came back the boys had finished and I had them setting the table for dinner. While we were eating, Tony asked. "Can you play chess, Dan?"

I watched him smile, then say. "I know a little bit about the game. Why?"

"Will you play chess with me and Jimmy after supper?"

★

I put the dishes in the dishwasher, then went to my bedroom to start cleaning Grandma's desk out. Though it didn't have much in it, it needed to be cleaned anyway. While I was in the bedroom, I took my bra off, then when I put my blouse back on I left the top two buttons open. I thought about leaving more of them open, but I was afraid the boys would notice.

I don't know how long I was in the bedroom, but I'd finished cleaning the desk. Suddenly, Tony was near me, and said. "Mom. Dan's really smart."

"Is he?"

"Yes. He's been showing Jimmy and me how to play better chess. I asked him if he could teach me to play better chess all of the time?"

I looked at him. There was a question yet to come. "And?"

"Well. . . he said he could but I'd have to ask you if it would be okay?"

"Well of course it would be okay, but why would you have to ask?"

"Cause, Dan said it would take about a year to really learn the fundamentals."

I smiled, "But, honey. Dan doesn't live around here."

"I don't know Mom. That's what he said."

After the boys went to bed, I was sitting across the table from Dan. I had my blouse open as far as I could go without being to obvious.

Dan looked over at me, his eyes drifted to my open blouse, he smiled, but said. "Annie, I'm bushed. I need some sleep. I started my day about four thirty this morning and I'm spent. Though I'd rather look at you, I have to get some sleep."

"Okay. Go for it. I've got to stay up awhile yet so I don't mess up my daily routine. Is there a particular time you want to get up in the morning?"

"No. Not tomorrow. I'll sleep until I wake up."

This morning I'd fixed the boys breakfast and their lunches, and then they were gone on their way to school. So far this morning I had spent most of the time thinking of how Dan looked in the shower, and I couldn't stand it any longer. I went to his bedroom door, opened it, and walked over to the side of the bed. Apparently I'd made just enough noise, because his eyes opened, and he said.

"Morning."

I pulled my nightshirt up over my head, then leaned over. With my left hand resting on the edge of the bed, I reached down to take my right slipper off. Making sure my breasts moved around so he could see them jiggling. Then I changed hands and took off my other slipper. I made sure I bounced around enough to excite him, then I said, "Move over."

When he'd moved, I climbing along side of him. I pushed my breasts against him and my right hand found his hard prick swelling. I stroked him slowly while he pulled at my nipple. Lifting my breast up, then dropping it. I said. "Move over some more."

He moved, and I moved over too. Then I lay on my back and opened my legs. I could feel his long shaft dragging up over my leg, and I said. "Dan. I haven't had a prick in me in a long time. So go slow and easy at first. Okay?"

He smiled down at me as he said. "I understand what you are telling me. I am long and I will take it easy."

When Dan was up over me, he wet his fingers, then moved them to the end of his prick. I felt him opening me with his fingers, and he started to push into me. I bit my lip but kept quiet as he pried me open. Then I enjoyed every fucking inch of him as he filled me. First it was a couple of inches, then he backed out. Slightly. Then a couple of inched deeper on the next penetration. Then out, then in deeper. God, when he finally rested on top of me, I was so full of him I couldn't believe I actually had that much inside of me.

"Fuck, Annie. You feel damn good. You're pussy is tight though so I may not be able to last as long as I like." Then he started fucking me. I was so excited by his long strokes it didn't take me long to cum. He was pulling out slowly, out, out, out, out, then in, in, in, in. Then out, out, out, out, then in, in, in. As each inch came back into me I savored every part of him. And, I came again. When Dan lunged deep into me and ground his prick deep in me, I knew he was cumming. I could feel the warmth of his flow, then his balls resting between my legs.

After a few moments as we savored the pleasure from one another, he moved off of me and as he lay beside me, I said. "Dan, I have to get some sleep now, because this is my night time."

"Okay."

"Stay here and then fuck me again when I wake up?"

"So, you like cock, huh?"

I smiled, I called it a prick, he calls it his cock. "Yes. I like cock and I want more of it."

I woke a couple of hours later to find Dan's hands exploring me. He had raised up on his elbow and had his hand down between my legs. When I opened my eyes, he said. Damn, that pussy feels good to my fingers. You have nice fleshy lips and I want to taste you later, Okay?"

"Taste me?"

"Yes. You know lick your clit with my tongue."

"Oh God, Dan. I've heard about that, but I've never experienced it. I know nothing about oral sex."

"Well, we will see to your education. But, for now, I want to suck on your nipples, then fuck you again."

I smiled and said. "I think I'm stretched open enough now you can just fuck my brains out. I am already wet thinking of that nice thick cock fucking me."

Then, his mouth started sucking on my nipples and his finger was rubbing my clit. I came with the pleasure of both, and I said. "Dan, fuck me. NOW."

We showered together, washed each other, then dried off and headed for the kitchen to get something to eat. I fixed us a sandwich and as we finished eating, Dan said. "Go get a pillow and a small blanket of some kind."

I went to get them but at the moment I had no idea what he wanted them for, but I knew I was going to enjoy whatever it was. When I came back, he had my table pulled out into the center of the kitchen with three chairs at one end. I handed him the blanket and he spread it out over the top of the table, then he took the pillow from me and put it on one end of the table. Next he moved two chairs to the corners of the table at the one end, then said. "Climb up here."

When I was up on the table, he put my feet on the chairs at the corner, then he moved the other one up close to the table, but between my legs and I was already getting wet with anticipation. He rubbed his hands up and down the inside of my thighs, then I could feel his thumbs pulling my pussy open. When his tongue touched my clit I could feel my legs tightens with the sudden unexpected pleasure. It was only moments before I said. "OH, fuck, Dan. Ohhh, fuucck. Ohhh, Fucckk, Oh my God that's good." Then just a few moments later, I told him. "I'm going to cum, Dan. Right fucking now. OOOOHhhh, FFFuuuc. . . " I felt my whole body quiver from the intense climax.

As I lay recovering, Dan dried his face, with tissues from a counter nearby. Then he came around to where my head was on the table and said. "Wet me." As his hand came to my head I understood and turned my face toward his hard cock, When he moved to my lips, I opened my mouth, and did I ever get him wet. I swirled my tongue around the end of his cock feeling the ridge on the back of his cock head and the hole where his cum comes out. But, suddenly he pulled out of me and walked down to the other end of the table. I heard the chair being moved back and as I looked down toward Dan, his left hand reached down and opened my pussy. I could see his right arm move as he guided his cock into me. Then, he pushed into me all in one stroke. I fucking near came right then. He didn't fuck me slowly this time. He just got into a fuck rhythm. I came just before Dan did, but he stayed in me for a short time. While we were both coming down from the sexual peak, I said. "Dan."

"Yes."

"I liked the feel of you in my mouth."

"Good, we'll do it again then."

We went to my bathroom and washed up, then we
got dressed. I would rather stay naked, but I knew
my boys would be home in a few short hours. As it
was shortly after we were dressed that, Dan said.
"Can I use your car?"

"Sure."

"Good. I have an interview after while at the
airport."

"An interview at the airport?"

"Yeah. I read an article in your paper that said they
are doubling the size of all of the facilities out
there, and I am a certified jet engine mechanic.
They want to talk to me."

When the boys got home, one of the first things
they said was. "Where's Dan, Mom?"

I explained what was going on, when Tony said.
"Where's he gonna live, Mom?"

"I don't know. Why?"

"We could rent him our other bedroom, then he
could teach us how to play chess every day."

"Well . . we'll see what happens."

Dan came home just as dinner was almost over, but I had saved him something to eat. He sat at the table, smiled, then said. "I start work in two weeks."

Jimmy said, "We are going to rent you our extra bedroom."

Dan smiled, and. "Are you now?"

"Yeah, if Mom says it's okay."

Dan turned to me, and I replied. "If you like, and if we can agree on a price to be paid."

★

Later and after the kids had gone to bed, Dan said. "I've gotta get some sleep I have a long drive tomorrow."

"How long will you be gone?"

"About a week. I don't have a lot of stuff yet. I haven't been out of the navy long enough to have acquired much."

He kissed me goodnight, but there was a lot of desire in that kissing. After Dan went into his bedroom, I went to mine and started setting up my stuff in Grandma's old desk. I'd left my bedroom door slightly ajar, but soon heard light tapping sound. I turned to see Dan peeking around the edge of the door. "I couldn't sleep."

"Come in."

He came in and I could see he was barefoot and only had his boxer shorts and a Tee shirt on. He pushed my door back to an almost closed position and asked. "Will the boys wake up if we make any noise?"

"No. They are very sound sleepers."

"Good, because. . . " I watched as he went over to my bed, pulled his shorts off and got on top of the bed. He lay with his legs open and his cock hard. Then he continued. "You remember our conversation this afternoon about oral sex? Well now It's your turn."

I closed the lid on my laptop computer and went over to him. I got undressed and climbed up on the bed. When I was ready, he told me, "Get comfortable and if you can lean up over me." So I moved and when I was ready I asked. "What do I do?"

"You need to Keep your teeth out of the way, then pull my foreskin down with your fingers and simply fuck me with your mouth."

"You'll tell me when to stop then?"

"Oh, you'll know when to stop."

I was surprised by how nice it felt to have him in my mouth again. I started slowly until I felt comfortable in what I was doing, and when Dan said. "Go a little faster."

I spent a little while sucking his cock, but I felt his ass move up to me, and I heard him groan loudly, then he squirted his cum into my mouth, I swallowed without thinking, and I sucked him some more to kind of dry him off, then I lifted off of him and asked. "Did I do okay?"

"You did damn good. So, what do you think of oral sex?"

"I think we should do it often."

"Good, but now lets fuck."

Dan sucked my nipples until he was hard and I moved up over him. I was wet enough that I could just slip down over his cock. As I settled down on him, I sat up straight. I heard him say something like. "God your tits feel good." And I could feel his hands on me, but I was paying attention to how my pussy felt. I was bottomed out on him and he was very deep inside me. I was so full of cock, and being impaled on him opened me wide enough that I felt his every inch to the extent that even just moving around a little bit brought me up to my peak and I fucking came just sitting there. After I came, I had to lean over, or fall, but Dan held me and said. "No, Annie. You have to finish fucking me."

Feeling his cock in me helped me recover quickly and by the time I got Dan off I had come again twice. As we rested, he said. "You get off easy don't you?"

"I do with you." After Dan had left me to go back to his bedroom, I planned on how I would wake him in the morning. I'd suck him up hard, then get on top of him, and fuck him.

DARK OF NIGHT
Larry sleeps very soundly. I mean, very soundly.
He does wake up when his alarm goes off in the
morning, but he sleeps through most everything
else. And, I kinda like this, but let me tell you why.
I'm a woman who really likes sex, so I get excited
easily. Recently when I got up one night to go to
the bathroom and when I came back to beds I
cuddled up to Larry to get warm, and because he
was lying on his back I reached down to take his
cock in my hand. I suppose he's always been this
way and I just never paid any attention to it, but
now it surprised me. When I wrapped my hand
around his cock, it started to kinda pulse, or move
around a little bit.

Intrigued, I put my thumb on one side of his cock
and two fingers on the other side, then I started
stroking him slowly. It wasn't an instant reaction,
but his cock started to get hard. Damn, the idea of
my playing with his cock while he was asleep,
stirred me between the legs. I took it easy, but I
lifted the covers off of his waist and his crouch.
Then I moved down further on the bed. I had to be
careful not to lean over onto him, but I was able to
slip my mouth over his cock and suck on it. Fuck
this was exciting and with the feel of him in my
mouth, I fucking climaxed after a short time. I
dried him with my mouth as best I could, then
moved back up on the bed and covered us up.
Pleased with myself, I went to sleep.

When the alarm went off in the morning, Larry shut it off, turned up on his side and reached for me. His hand feeling my tits, then suddenly, he pulled the covers off of us, and said. "Move your ass over here."

I was startled. "What?"

"You heard me. Move your fucking ass over here."

I moved toward him, and he moved up over me and between my legs. He wet his cock, and more than he usually does, then he reached down to open me and he shoved his hard shaft all the way into my pussy. He never pushes all the way into on the first stroke. He usually takes two or three strokes before he's all the way in me. But not this time. This time I felt his cock invading my pussy, as if it mattered if I was ready or not.

"Larry, What. . . "

"Sshhussh. Just be quiet. I'm so fucking horny this morning that I'm gonna fuck you right now."

Larry pounded into me. Jarring my clit on each of his down plunges. Jamming his cock deep into me. After a few minutes he dropped heavily on top of me and I knew he was cumming. I had already reached my peak and climaxed. It was different this time, though. I had just laid there and felt it

climbing up to my pussy, then it just happened.
While Larry shaved and showered, I got up to fix
his breakfast and a lunch to take with him to work.
After he'd gone for the day, I thought about what
had happened. I figured that if I could suck his
cock at night, and get off, then get a good fucking
pounding the next morning, I'd do it a couple of
times a month. At least, maybe more. God that was
a good fuck he gave me this morning.

FRED. BILL & JACKIE

It was quiet between the two of us as we sat having
a beer together on Bill's patio. I figured something
was bothering, Bill. I said.

"You're awfully quiet today, Bill. Something
bothering you?"

He shifted on his deck chair, but didn't look at me
as he replied. "Nah. Nothin."

I knew better, so I pushed him a bit. "Bullshit.
Something got you worked up. Was it your last
medical treatment?" I knew he had treatments a
couple of times a month, and sometimes they
bothered his for a few days. This takes place in the
city, about a three hour drive from here.

He finally looked over at me, then started. "No, it's
not that. It's Jackie. I can't give her what she needs
now. I just can't get it up and keep it up any more."

"Ahh, I see." I too was fast approaching the same
dilemma.

"I just don't know what to do about it?"

"So, what if she had a fiend in need."

"A what?"

"Someone who can give her what she wants, but with no strings attached."

"Are you kidding me?"

"Not at all."

I knew he'd think on this for a spell, so I let it alone. I think it must have been a couple of days before he called me late at night. He asked. "This friendship thing you were telling me about. How would I go about doing this?"

I explained about using the internet to make arrangements, but he didn't like the idea of doing that. I also added. Of course you should talk to Jackie about this kind of thing as well. Maybe she'll have an idea."

"Okay. I'll get back to you. I have an idea I'd like to ask you about."

It was a week later when Bill had asked me over to their place. He, Jackie and I were sitting in his living room. Jackie had just given each of us an iced tea, then she sat on the same couch I was sitting on. Bill was in a chair across from me, and he started the conversation as to why he had asked me over. "Fred. Jackie and I have discussed the problem about her physical needs and my ability to fulfill her desires."

I was curious, of course, but I only asked. "So. Have you come up with a direction to go in?"

"We have. And we want your opinion about what we decided on."

"And that is?"

Jackie leaned toward me as she said. "We think you are our best choice."

I was shocked. I simply didn't know how to respond at the moment. "Oh my God. You want to use me as the friend?"

Jackie said. "We'll let you think on it for a spell. :If you don't like the idea, don't worry about it. I have a toy to use when I like."

I'd stayed for dinner and Jackie was very attentive to me during the course of the meal. To the point of leaning over me to freshen my glass of wine. I could not help but look down her dress to see some decent cleavage. I was nervous, but Bill didn't seem to notice what was going on.

It was a week and a half later, during the time of night that I knew bill watched one of his favorite television programs that my phone rang.

"Hello?"

"Fred. Can you come see me tomorrow morning? After ten?"

I could hear Bill's program going in the background. "I guess so."

"Please, Fred. Please."

"Okay. I'll see you in the morning."

When I arrived at their house the next morning, I was thinking this could be the day. I had showered and shaved just for that possibility, and when Jackie opened the door I was pretty sure I had guessed right. She had a long Tee shirt on, one that came down nearly to her knees. I was pretty sure that was all she had on.

"Bill's gone into the city for a treatment."

"Okay."

"Which means we have hours to play/"

I knew I was expected to go to bed with her, and I have to admit I was looking forward to doing just that. It had been almost the only thing I had been thinking about for the past few days. "So, how do you want to start with us?"

"I have fresh coffee ready. We can sit at the table to talk a bit. Okay?"

"Sure."

I sat in a chair by the round table. She sat in one right next to mine. Well close anyway. We were almost done with our coffee when Jackie stood up, crossed her arms, and lifted the Tee shirt up and over her head. Then she laid it down on the seat of the chair she'd been sitting on. "I"ll freshen our coffee."

I watched her ass as she walked away to get the coffee pot. Then I glanced down at the Tee shirt. Without thinking, I said. "Jackie. There's a damp spot on the bottom of your Tee shirt."

As she walked back toward me, I could see her tits moving back and forth and with a slight bounce to them as well.

She replied. "I'm not surprised by the wet spot. I get very wet when I'm about to get naked in front of a man I want to fuck me."

"Jackie. You look damn good naked."

"Yes, well now it's your turn. Push your chair back, then take your clothes off and put them on the chair on the other side of the table."

When she got to me she leaned over to pour our coffee and her tits were hanging down right in front of my face.

"Damn your tits look good."

"You want to feel them and suck on them?"

"Of course."

She took the coffee pot back, but on the way she said. "Move your chair out a bit further from the table."

She made a point of swinging her tits from side to side when she walked back, but this time she came over to me and stepped over my legs. Then she sat down on my lap. When she was comfortable, she leaned back against the table and rested on her elbows. Her tits pushed out for me. I didn't waste any time. I reached up with my hands and with my thumbs under her tits, my fingers were up around the outside edges and slightly over the top. I was holding them like bottles. I moved my mouth over to her right nipple first and sucked on it. Her hands moved behind my head and she pulled me into her tighter. I sucked on that nipple for a bit, then changed to the other one.

She pulled her nipple out of my mouth as she started to stand up. "Fred. The feeling of your hard cock rubbing against my wet lips is too much. We need to go to bed. Now. Right fucking now."

She led me to her guests' bedroom and then she laid down in the center of the bed. I said. "Jackie, Move over."

"You don't want me in the middle?"

"Not to begin with."

She moved over to one side and I laid down along side of her. But with my cock up near her tits and her pussy near my chest. Then I pulled her leg up over my arm so that it was resting against my elbow. I must have surprised her because she said.

"Why are we this way?"

"Because I want to look at and feel your pussy."

"Oh God. I like the idea of you looking closely at my pussy."

I reached in between her legs and began to rub her inner thighs. When my finger tips touched her lips, she shuddered. "Oh God, Fred. Fuck that feels good."

I leaned over to lick her with my tongue and she made an unexpected movement. "Oh. That feels good."

"Can you get off this way?" I asked.

"I. . . .I don't know?"

"You don't know if you can climax with a man using his tongue on your pussy?"

"No. I don't."

I got up off the bed and had her move into the center. Then I went down to the end of the bed and crawled up between her legs. When I pushed her open with my tongue and found her clit, her hands came down to pull my face into her.

It took a while, but it paid off. To the point that she was making noises and her body was bucking up to try to get some cock in her as I worked her pussy with my tongue and my whole mouth. I was paying attention to what I was doing and was not listening to her words, but I knew they were words of heat. Then, suddenly, she fell into a complete state of relaxation. She did not move. I looked up to see her eyes closed, her mouth open, but not speaking.

"Jackie. You okay?"

"Oh God. I am very okay. In all of my life I've never had a climax as intense as that."

I got up off the bed and went to the bathroom. I washed my face with a warm wet washcloth, then after rinsing it, I went was washed between her legs as well. When I came back, I laid down along side of her. My left leg up over hers, and using my hands I was feeling her tits.

We laid there awhile, then she said. "Fred."

"Yes."

"Fuck me now."

I moved up on top of her and nestled between her legs. As I felt my cock lying against the lips to her pussy, I simply raised some and drug it back and forth over her lips. It was only moments before I entered her without our hands helping. She was wet and ready for me. I started to just lie on her and feel her, but she said.

"Don't tease me, Fred. Fuck me."

It didn't take long before she came to a climax and when she did, I moved my hands down under her and began to fuck her for myself. That too, didn't take long. As we lay together on top of the bed, she said.

"I've never been fucked that way before."

"You mean with a man on top?"

"NO. No, I mean the way you did it. You put all of your weight on top of me, then slid your hands down under the cheeks of my ass. You held me in place to fuck me. It made me feel like a 'Fuck' prisoner."

"I'm sorry. You should have told me it made you feel trapped."

"Oh, no. I didn't feel trapped. I fucking enjoyed it that way. You were so busy banging into me at the last that you probably didn't notice I climaxed again. It was so quick and so unexpected that I just felt myself cum."

About a half hour later we were up, but naked, having a small lunch in her kitchen. Jackie said. "When you used your tongue on me I wondered why Tom and I have never had oral sex before?"

I replied. "Well, not everybody enjoys oral sex."

"Apparently you do."

"Very much."

"The next time you come to see me. I'll suck on you. Would you like that?"

"I'm fucking horny just thinking about it. Let's go fuck once more before I have to go home."

We took more time this last time. There wasn't any real need to get off, just to feel each other as we fucked. After we washed up, and I got dressed, she walked me to her front door. She was still naked and looked damn good. She stood in the open doorway as I walked out. At the last minute she said.

"Fred. The next time you can come to me, call me just before you leave your house. Then when you get here, I'll be waiting for you just like this. Naked in the doorway and hungry for you."

God that was a picture I was going to keep in my mind. Hopefully it wouldn't be too long until this happened again.

FRIENDS

John and I were in my kitchen, and putting our
empty wine glasses in the sink. We were naked as
usual. Suddenly someone knocked at my front
door. John said. "Are we expecting someone?"

"No. You stay here. I'll go see who it is."

I grabbed my robe from the back of a chair and
pulled it on over my shoulders and held it together
with my hand. Then went to look through the peep
hole in the door. I whispered to John. "It's my
friend, Jane."

I opened the door to tell her that I was busy and
would see her later, but she pushed in past me
saying. "Let me in. It's cold out here."

She headed straight to my couch in the living room
and sat on the far end. By the time I caught up with
her, my robe had fallen open. Jane looked up at me
and saw I was nude, then said. "Oh. I'm sorry were
you about to . . . .OHH my God."

Now she saw John standing in my kitchen, but
only from the waist up. And, of course he didn't
appear to have anything on. "Why didn't you tell
me you had company?"

"Jane, you didn't give me a chance to tell you."

"Oh. I'm sorry. I better leave."

"By now it didn't really matter. She knew John and I were going to fool around. So I said. "No. Sit still."

I turned to John and said. "You might as well come out here."

"Are you sure?"

"Yes." I patted the couch between Jane and I, and said. "Sit right here."

When John sat between us, he put one arm up on the back of the couch and around my shoulders, the other one went up behind Jane's shoulders. His legs were open and his cock, though not completely hard, was hanging down between his legs.

I said. "Jane, this is John."

I saw her looking down between John's legs as she said. "Hi, John."

I turned slightly and reached down to stroke John's cock with my thumb and two fingers as she watched.

When he came up hard, John raised his hand behind her head and pulled her mouth to his. I heard her moan slightly so I knew his tongue was in her mouth.

When he pulled away, he leaned close to her ear and whispered something to her. Then he sat back up. I looked over at her and asked. "What did he tell you?"

"I . . .Uh, he. . . .he said. Come suck it."

I smiled, then said. "Well, it's ready."

She didn't move for a few seconds. Then she got up off the couch, and moved over between John's legs and got down on her knees. As I watched her head bobbin up and down on his cock, I said. "John. We might as well go to bed. Don't you think?"

"Yes. We might as well."

Jane lifted her mouth up off of John, stood up and started unbuttoning her blouse as she headed for my bedroom. John was rubbing the cheeks of my ass as we followed her. I knew that Jane was so horny right now that I was not going to be the first one fucked.

When we got into my bedroom, Jane had already pulled the sheet and blanket down to the foot of the bed, and she was getting onto the bed. As she laid down, she said. "John. Fuck me first. Please, please, please."

John looked at me and I raised an eyebrow and shrugged a shoulder, as if to say. "Whatever." He shrugged his shoulder back to me and moved over to the other side of the bed. As he moved over Jane, I was climbing onto the bed on the near side. I watched her reach down to open her hairy pussy, and to guide John into her. I know John likes my pussy a lot, and part of that is because I shave it for him.

As I watched him fucking her I became aware of things I'd never paid much attention to before. I watched his ass raise up just before he slammed down into her. And when he hammered her, her whole body shifted on the bed, then settled back where it had been just before his next stroke. I know that when he plunges into me, it jars me too. I just didn't realize how much movement takes place. And when he hits my clit on his hard downstroke, it forces my climax up a bit, then the next stroke brings it up another notch, until I fucking get off.

I also heard his cock making a kind of "slluusshing, or sluurrping" noise as he pulled out of her to get ready for his next hammering plunge. I don't think it makes that sound when he fucks me. I'm not sure but maybe it happens if Jane is a really wet fuck.

After Jane came, John pulled out of her and I could see his cock was wet. He walked into the bathroom and I heard him washing himself. When he came back, he came around to me. I lay on my back and Jane moved over so we would have room. John mounted me, slipped his cock into me, and started fucking me. He didn't fuck me fast, nor as hard as he had fucked Jane. He was going to fuck me slowly and enjoy me. And I was damn well going to let him.

FRUSTRATIONS
Many of us suffer from frustrations. Often they are
similar in scope. Mine is because I am a large
woman and as so, it is difficult to find a man who
can fuck me, in any position. Another one,
according to an old guy I know, is aging. He once
told me that between his age, and his medications,
he couldn't get a hard on and keep it long enough
to fuck a woman. He can keep it long enough to
masturbate, but that's about it. Jimmy, has in the
past, on more than one occasion brought me to a
climax, though not by fucking me. Still, pleasure is
pleasure. So, yesterday he came to visit me, at my
invitation. Here's what I did with him when he
arrived.

I met him wearing a button down dress with most
of the buttons undone so that he could see most of
my tits when he looked down the front of my
dress, which he did.

"Damn, you look good."

I undid a few more buttons, then said. "Why don't
you enjoy them?"

He opened my dress and took my tits into his
hands, then began sucking on my nipples. First
one, then the other, and he pinched them because
he knows this turns me on quickly.

Not that I wasn't already hot and moist. When he finally let them go, I stepped back a bit, and while he watched I got undressed.

"Well fuck, Marilyn."

"I know you can't fuck me, but you can lick me."

"Yes. I can." I took him by the hand and led him to my bedroom. While he got undressed I got up on my bed and spread my legs so he could get to my clit. He kissed me on my thighs as moved up between my legs, then when his tongue reached me, I shuddered with the touch. Jimmy's patient, so he took his time to bring me up to my peak and I called out to him. "Oh fuck, oh fuck I'm cumming Jimmy. Oh fuck yes. . . .Now, right fucking . . . .Uhhh, Uhh. Ahhh. Oh God that was good."

After I recovered, I said. "Jimmy, move up here higher on the bed."

After he was where I wanted him, I put a pillow next to his leg for me to rest my shoulder on, then I lay my head on his hip. I reached up with my hand and slowly started stroking his cock with two fingers and my thumb. As he came up I changed to my full hand around him and stroked him slowly. As he began to move up with my hand strokes,

leaned over and took the head of his cock in my
mouth, and he moaned with the pleasure. I kept
this up until he came in my mouth.

His hand came down to rest on my head and he
said. "Marilyn. You are so fucking good at sucking
cock. Thank you."

The point is, no matter what it is that keeps you
from enjoying yourself sexually, it can be
overcome in some manner. You just have to find
the right partner. So do it.

HANDS

It's just this thing I have about men's hands. I love big hands on a man, and when I look at men it's their hands that are what I look at first. Maybe I'm different from many women, but I fantasize when I see a man with big hands. Let me give you an idea of what I mean.

I think of the man standing in front of me and I'm naked from head to toe. He lifts one of my tits up by the nipple while his other hand is rubbing and feeling my tit on all sides, then hefting the weight of it. He then moves to my other tit and does the same thing and I want him to suck on them. And, I love it when his hands take hold of my nipples and swing my tits around while he watches them moving.

I imagine him going behind me and rubbing the cheeks of my ass as he works his way around me and his cock rubbing against my cheeks as he moves up tight to me and his hands going up under my arms to hold my tits in each hand. His cock now resting between my cheeks. He whispers fuck talk into my ear as he kisses me on the neck. After he lets go of my tits and he moves his hands down my sides he says things to me like, "Open your legs."

As his hands are rubbing my inner thighs, my pussy is screaming for his touch. He comes back around in front of me and kneels on the floor in front of me. His hands move over my hips and down to work their way in between my now wide open legs. As he works his way upward I am so fucking wet with want that when his fingers do get to my pussy he cups my mound with one hand and begins to rub my lips. As he searches for my clit, I fucking near cum.

I'M NOT DONE YET

I was in the supermarket a couple of weeks ago, and as I came around the end of the wine aisle I saw a younger man looking at a bottle of wine. I looked down at my shopping list to see what else I wanted at the store, and when I looked back up I was almost to the man I'd seen before, only now he was looking at me. In fact I became aware he seemed to be waiting for me.

When I got close, he held a bottle of white wine up for me to see, and said. "Have you ever tasted a Riesling before?"

Surprised he would even ask me, I answered. "Yes. It's quite good."

He smiled at me as he said. "Good. When can we share this one?"

"What?"

"I'd like to share this bottle of wine with you. And then go. . . "

"I'm sorry. Do I know you?"

"I'm Dennis, and you are?"

I don't know why, but I said. "Marcie."

"Marcie, why don't we start over. There's a deli at the other end of the store. If you're not in a hurry, maybe we could get something and talk a bit?"

This guy was different, confident, apparently has a sense of humor, and we were in a public place, so I said. "Okay."

I got us a table while Dennis got me a spring roll and tea, and himself a chicken strip and a soda. After he sat down across from me we began to eat our stuff without saying anything. When Dennis finished his chicken strip he licked his finger tips then used the paper napkins to wipe his fingers clean. When I finished my spring roll I used the paper napkin to clean my fingers. As I picked up my tea, I laid my left hand down on the table top. Dennis put his left hand over the top of mine, then began to finish his soda. In my mind I felt odd, because what I was thinking of was that he was on top of me.

"Dennis you started to tell me about going somewhere before I interrupted you."

"Hummppff, Oh, yes. I want to go to bed with you."

I didn't reply to what he'd said, so we talked some more. Long enough that we had a refill on our drinks.

Finally he asked. "You do live around here, don't you Marcie?"

"Yes. I live in one of the Lakeside Condo's. Where do you live?"

"I have a small apartment in the Wayside Complex. Are you open to discussing our going to bed together?"

"Dennis. I'm an old woman. I'm not much to look at any longer, and I haven't been to bed with a man in years."

"Well, Marcie. I'm an old man, and I haven't been to be with a woman in much to long. But, we could share a glass of wine and talk about it?"

"I have to think about that."

"Okay. So tell me where you live and I can stop by on say, Wednesday to see you?"

I decided, to some degree. Dennis, from my condo I can look out over the lake in the front, and the parking lot in the back. So, if I decide to share a bottle of wine with you, I'll leave a piece of paper taped up in my back window on Wednesday. You will be able to see it from the parking lot and you will know where to find me.?"

"Wonderful."

We chatted a bit longer, then we both finished our shopping. I purchased a bottle of Riesling wine to take with me just in case. When Wednesday came, I made a mistake. I thought it was Tuesday, so when I actually put the piece of paper in my window, it was Thursday. At the end of the day I was disappointed that Dennis hadn't come by. It wasn't until the ten O'clock news that I realized my error. I had lost a day. I meant to go take the paper down, but forgot to do that at the time.

Then, Last week I heard someone knocking at my door in the early afternoon. When I peeked through peephole in the door, I saw him. I opened the door, and said. "Dennis. Please come in."

Inside he said. "I made a mistake. I thought you meant last week, so when I came by on Wednesday, I couldn't see a piece of paper in anyone's window. So, today I just took a chance and drove through your parking lot, and was very pleased to see a window with a piece of paper in it."

"I'm glad you saw it and stopped to see me." He surprised me by reaching up and putting his hand on my cheek, then he kissed me lightly.

I was flustered, well I liked it, but still I wasn't
ready for that to happen. I took his hand and led
him to the kitchen. In there I went to the
refrigerator and took out the bottle of wine. I
handed it to him and said. "In that last drawer over
there you'll find a corkscrew.

If you'll get our wine ready, then take it and that
bowl of crackers on the counter there, into the
living room, I'll get our snacks ready."

While he was removing the foil from the bottle and
opening it. I got the dish with the cheese, pickle
slices and cold cuts ready. We both headed for my
couch. With the things placed on the coffee table,
Dennis poured us a glass of wine. We sipped wine,
munched the snacks, but only talked about my
view of the lake. All things but what we intended
to talk about. Finally I had an idea. I said. "Dennis.
I have to admit that this time of day I usually take a
nap."

"Me too. I just figured I'd miss it today."

"Well. . . we could go take one now?"

"That's a wonderful idea."

After we put the leftovers back in the refrigerator,
and the wine had the cork shoved back into the
bottle, I led him to my bedroom.

Inside I said. "I like to sleep on the right side."

"Okay. That's good for me."

I Pointed to a chair on his side and said. "You can put your clothes on that chair over there."

As we got undressed, we both took glances at one another. It was apparent that we were both older people. I skin was not tight like youngsters, but it didn't matter. I climbed into bed on my side and Dennis came over close to me. I kissed him lightly, and said. "How long do you nap?"

"About an hour, usually."

"I might sleep a bit longer, so I'll see you when we wake up." I don't think he was disappointed in having to wait. He just pulled the covers up to his chin and closed his eyes.

When I woke awhile later, Dennis was up on his elbow and against my right side, his arm laying across me and his right hand cupping my boob. His thumb was rubbing my nipple. I could feel the nipple springing back up to an erect position after his thumb moved off of it. It sent a sensation into my very core. I turned flat onto my back and let my right hand find his cock.

It was nearly hard and it pulsed in my hand when I squeezed it lightly. As he moved his hand down between my legs, I opened them without even thinking about doing that. It just seemed natural.

Dennis leaned over and kissed me, then said. "Hi, sleepy head."

I grinned at him and said. "Hi, yourself. Why don't we use this?" And I squeezed his cock again.

He moved up over me, then when he was between my legs. He reached his fingers to his mouth, then wet his cock. I reached down at the same time he did and we both opened me. He started to push into me but it took him four short strokes to finally get all of the way in. I mean I've not had a man in me in a long time so it took a bit for me to really get good and wet.

We both enjoyed the feeling of fucking. Dennis said. "Damn, Marcie. You feel wonderful. It si so good to feel your warm wet pussy surrounding me."

Then he fucked me slowly. Very slowly, as if to feel every bit of me inside. I don't know how long we did it that way, but finally I could feel the urgency to go all of the way. "Dennis, fuck me a bit faster now."

He started going a little faster, but I asked him. "Can you go a little faster, yet?"

"Yes, but if I do, I'm gonna cum."

"Then, cum, Dennis. Fuck me and cum in me."

I came, but only just before Dennis did. We lay there entwined for a few moments, then when Dennis moved off of me and down to my side, I felt his wet cock slipping across my upper leg. Wet from both of us. A good fucking, wetness. We went into my bathroom and we washed ourselves, then, still naked, we went to get the rest of the wine and snacks. Between his sips of wine, Dennis would put his glass down, and feel my tits. Tugging at my nipples, lifting me, then letting them fall back down. "I like your tits, Marcie."

"If you lay your head in my lap, you could suck on them."

He finished his glass of wine, and was able to lay down on the couch. His knees were doubled up, but he fit okay. I helped him get comfy, and leaned in such a way so that he could suck on my nipples. I really liked the feeling it was giving me, and I watched his cock harden up quickly. I r reached out to hold it in my hand, but it made me so needy, that I said. "Dennis, trade me places."

When I had Dennis where I wanted him, I leaned over him, and put my hands on the back of the couch so that he could still suck on my nipples, but also so I could straddle him and sit on his hard cock. As I slipped down over him, he felt much deeper in me than in bed. I haven't climaxed at all in a long time, but today, with Dennis and his cock, I was enjoying a long forgotten pleasure. Just sitting on his, and feeling him deep in me brought a sexual spasm that rocked me. Fuck I had a intense climax. Dennis knew what had happened, and he said.

"Marcie, get the fuck off of me and get your ass on the floor."

I lay down on my thick carpeting, and Dennis pushed his cock into my pussy and fucked me hard and fast. I could hardly believe it, but I came again. Shortly after I came, Dennis drove hard into me as far as he could go, and he filled me with his cum again.

In the coming weeks, Dennis and I cut out pubic hair short and tried oral sex, that was fun too. He fucked me on my kitchen table, and out on my small terrace overlooking the lake late one night. God that seemed strange. To fuck outside, but we both liked the danger of possibly being caught out there screwing. Now, anytime we are together and in need, we only talk to each other in nasty sexual language. I mean, like he will tell me. "Marcie, lets go fuck." And once he did it while we were having lunch in a restaurant, and the waitress heard him.

As we left, she smiled at me and said. "Have a good time in bed."

I smiled back and said. "Well, it might be in bed, but it could be anywhere. We haven't tried the park yet."

I AM, THE WAY I AM.

I've never thought of myself as different, but sometimes when I talk about sex to other women, I think maybe I am different. Not all of them, mind you, but a few of them leave me feeling this way. So, here's the thing. As a rule I can take sex, or leave it. I simply don't care whether or not I fuck some guy. Don't misunderstand, there are men who fucking turn me on easily. Like the guy on the terrace, but we'll come back to that.

It's been my experience that younger guys aren't worth a crap in bed. In my case I know they like my big tits, but when the first one of these young dudes came onto me, and I went to bed with him, he fucked me much too fast and didn't last worth a damn.

Afterwards, he thought he would make some polite conversation and it consisted of his feeling about snow boarding, fast cars, and for Pete's sake, baseball cards. Jeeez, what a bust. The next young guy was pretty much the same. So that's it for young guys.

One time I tried an old guy. Old enough that he had to struggle to keep it up and he did all he could to see I reached a climax. He was really good with his tongue. These old guys deserve a try, but you have to remember they are old.

I'm of an age where I have a few years ahead of me that I can experiment with "Older men." And, like most other women, I've found these are the guys who are the best in bed. They can last awhile and they know how to fuck a woman. I've even found one or two who brought me up to more than one climax.

So, there's this guy I came across on the terrace of a friend's big place in the country. It was a warm night and during a party. It was very dark outside until your eyes became accustomed to the light outside. He was standing near the railing on a far corner of the terrace, smoking. I knew he heard me coming because he turned to look at me, and said. "Well, Hello."

I stopped by his side and said. "Hello, yourself. What are you doing out here by your lonesome?"

"Waiting for you."

I was surprised, and said. "Me?"

"Yes. You're wearing sweats, like myself."

"I'm not the only one around here wearing sweats. It seems to be the dress code around here."

He asked. "Are you bashful, or daring?"

"Well, I'm not bashful, and I may be somewhat daring."

"I'm glad."

He moved close to me and slipped his hand down inside my sweat pants to rub the cheeks of my ass. I was surprised, but I liked it too. Then, just as quickly he moved his hand around to the front of me and pushed his fingers down between my legs. "And, you're wet too."

I could see enough in the dim light that he was pulling his shorts down, and he said. "Pull your sweat pants down and lean over the railing."

For some reason, and it wasn't out of fear, I did as he said. When I was leaning over the railing, he swatted me on the ass and said. "Open."

I opened my legs as far as I could and in moments I could feel his nice hard cock pushing into me. He slammed into me, hard enough to bounce me back and forth on the railing. I had to hold on with my hands, but fuck he was damn good at screwing me.

I've talked to women who seem to love to fuck, and anytime and anyplace. They simply seem to love to fuck. I'm just not one of them.

LACY

I've known Frank for most of my life. He's been a friend of the family for years, and a guy who will help me with things when I ask, and I'd asked a few days ago. I asked him to come over to help me with something personal. He's an older guy, but in good shape, and sensitive to people. I tried to be ready for him then he'd gotten here. I'd gone over what I was going to say, and how I had dressed before he arrived. Just so you know, I was only wearing a blouse and skirt. Nothing else. I met him at the door and when I opened it he said. "Hi, Lacy." Not that I expected much more.

"Frank. Thanks for coming over."

"You said you needed some help with something?"

"Are you in a hurry, or do you have some time you can spend with me?"

"I can stay as long as you like. My time is pretty much my own these days."

Frank had sat down on my couch, and looked up at me expectantly. "So. How have you been?"

"I've been. . . . okay."

He kinda frowned. "Just okay?"

"Yeah. But. . . .I have this problem."

"Something I can help you with?"

"I hope so, Frank."

"What is it?"

I'd pulled my skirt hem up to my waist to show him my shaved pussy and opened my legs so he could see. Then I patted my mound and said. "I need some cock, Frank."

I could see it really surprised him. "Oh, damn, Lacy. Fuck that is beautiful, but. . . I'm a bit too old for you. . . and."

"Frank, can you still get it up?"

"Well, yes, but. . . .how long it will stay up is questionable"

"Then, Frank, let's get it up and fuck me with it. I mean it. I really need a good fuck."

"Jeez, Lacy. If anyone in the family ever found out about this, there would be hell to pay."

"Frank. The family will never find out. At least not from me. So, just so you know. I want you to fuck me every fucking day."

"Lacy, you know that can't happen?."
"Yes. I do know that. But I would like you to
screw me as often as we can arrange to be
together."

Then I took my skirt off and dropped it on the
coffee table. While he watched me. Then I started
unbuttoning my blouse. I dropped it on the table
with my skirt, then leaned over him by putting my
hands on the back of the couch near his shoulders,
and said. "And, Frank. These nipples need sucking
too."

As his hands reached for my tits, he moaned, then
said. "Well, dammit. Let go to bed and see how we
do with an old cock."

I was lying on my bed while Frank got undressed,
but he surprised me. He climbed up on the end of
the bed, and moved between my open legs. He lay
down, then pushed his hands up under the cheeks
of my ass, and started licking my clit. "Oh, damn,
Frank. Fuck that feels good." It didn't take him
long to get me off that way, then he moved up
between my legs and pushed his cock into my
pussy. He fucked me slowly and I know I came
twice before he shot his cum in me. After that we
lie on my bed talking, but as we talked, mostly
about sex, Frank was sucking on, or feeling my
nipples. I fucked him later in the day before he had
to leave.

Now, even though it's a few weeks later, When Frank comes to see me, he greets me in ways he knows will turn me on. Once in awhile he will pull my skirt up to my waist then smack me on the cheeks of the ass, then kiss me with a deep passion. Or, he may tell me to stay put in one place while he gets undressed as I watch. He may play with his cock while he stands in front of me with me sitting on my couch, or he may walk over to me when I'm naked and sitting on the couch, then put his hand on my head. This of course is to silently tell me to suck his cock. He may sit on my couch naked and have me get undressed while he watches me, or sit in such a way on my couch that tells me to lean over and suck him off. Sometimes he'll get down on the floor in front of me and lick my clit while I watch television. In bed he will take his time with my tits. Sucking on them, then pulling my nipples. Lifting them up then letting them go. Or he may push his cock into me while he is on his side and with me on my back and he's moved between my legs. Just moving enough to keep his cock hard, and me wanting more.

He is old enough to hinder his ability, but he is good to me sexually as much as he can be. When I do cum, it is usually with intensity. Fuck. He is good.

LOVE SYMBOLS
This comes from a story that took place around
1798 and in London England. Well, actually in a
small Hamlet not far from London. It seems that a
London writer, Charles, and artist, had an ongoing
affair with a woman he'd known for years. He
would arrange to take few days away on occasion
and in doing so he would send, Elizabeth a poste.

Actually a disguised invitation to join him at a
small cottage he kept on the edge of a lake. If she
could accompany him, she would meet him at a
predetermined location. He would have arranged
for a carriage and they would travel to his cottage
on the lake. Invariably when they arrived they
would make love straightaway. In fact they made
love at every opportunity.

On one of their retreats together, and after having
made love just before rising, Elizabeth announced.
"Charles, I'm going for a swim in the lake."

He watched as she left the cottage with only a
drying cloth draped around her neck.
Still, the physical beauty of her beckoned him. He
heard her dive into the water from a small dock at
which he kept a skiff, in which they would row
around in the nude on moonlit nights.

Aroused at the thought of seeing her walk around
nude, he himself went out to watch her swim.

When she saw him coming, and with a swollen member, she swam toward the dock.

As she neared him, he could see her head, and her buttocks. The rest of her was under the water and not clearly defined.

Suddenly he turned and left her there. When Elizabeth returned to the cottage, she found Charles drawing with a piece of charcoal on some art paper.

As she looked over his shoulder, she saw a small sketch he'd drawn. "What is this you've drawn here, Charlie?"

"It is a reminder of your beauty, and something I dearly love about you. You see when I gazed down upon you in the lake. I could see your head, of course, but when I looked further I saw the water forming a Vee between the cheeks of your buttocks, then going out and around to meet again in the small of your back."

The sketch Elizabeth was looking at looked like this. ♥

From that point on, when Charles would send Elizabeth a poste, he would end it with the heart-shaped sketch. In a sense, saying.

I love your sweet ass, and want to feel it again.

She would do the same on any returning poste to Charles. In a sense she was saying. "From the sweet ass you love so much."

One afternoon, as Elizabeth was entertaining lady friends, a note from Charles had been left out on her writing desk. Most of the note was covered by an envelope with the waxed seal on showing on top. But his ending sketch was open to view.

One of her friends saw the drawing and inquired. "Lizzy. What is this?"

Elisabeth, of course could not explain the real meaning behind the sketch. She said. "Oh. That's a symbol indicating a male friend's affection for me." Of course all of her friends then had to look at the sketch.

Soon after, they too, would send letters to those they were fond of, and would often use the heart-shaped sketch at the end of their letters to those they loved, or held affectionately in their memories.

Now you have an idea of how Valentines came about and the real meaning behind them.

MATTI

My sister, Matti, and I were in the small grocery store near our homes getting a couple of things. I was getting some tea bags and a newspaper. Matti was getting a quart of milk. While we were in the store, an old man came inside. I just called him old, I think he's younger than I am. I'd seen him around the area before, and he interested me. As I came around the end of a row of shelves, we nearly bumped into each other. He moved off to one side, and motioned with his hands, that I should go ahead of him. I did, and I liked him right away. His smile, and the look in his eyes as he looked at me felt kinda good. I thought he liked looking at me. I also had the feeling he was watching me walk ahead of him in the aisle as well.

As Matti and I got to our corner and turned to go up the hill to our places, I looked back and saw him coming out of the store and heading our way. When I reached the end of our walkway going into our apartment complex, I looked back down the hill and sure enough he was coming up our hill. We have a few tables on a patio outside our apartments and as I stopped there. I said. "Matti, I'm going to sit out here for a while and read my paper."

"Okay. I'll see you later." She started up the stairs
to her apartment. Stairs I'm glad I don't have to
climb, and because of that I live in the first unit on
the ground floor.

I was sitting at one of the patio tables facing the
street, and pretending to read my paper as he got to
our sidewalk. He paused there and saw me looking
his way, then he gave me a small wave. I waved
back, then he started going on up the hill. Just as
quickly he stopped and moved back to the end of
the sidewalk leading to where I was sitting and he
said something to me. I put my hand up behind my
ear, in a sense telling him I hadn't heard him. He
smiled and walked up to me. Then said. "Do you
have time to chat?"

"Sure I do."

Within a few minutes we learned each others
names and about each others life. That he was a
widower some four years, and that I was a widow
for six. Matti, my sister was a widow for a year
longer than I. Also that he lived in a Condo in the
next block up the street. When we came to a lull in
our conversation, Jonathan said. "Well. I suppose I
should let you get back to your paper."

I did what seemed the right thing at the moment.
"Jonathan, do you like tea?"

"Sure."

"Would you like to come in and have some tea, with me?"

"I'd like that very much."

While Jonathan sat at my kitchen table, I was trying to figure out how to make the next move without seeming to be too forward. Nothing was coming to me. I poured us some tea and sat near him. He asked me what I did most of the time, which isn't much. But, among the things I told him was an interest in chess. Though I could seldom find players near enough to play often.

He sat up straighter, "You play chess?"

"Yes. It's a wonderful game and time goes so quickly while you're playing."

"Do you have a chess set?"

"Of course."

"Well, let's play a few games then."

Later, I saw Jonathan look at his watch, then say. "My goodness, Marti. I've taken up your entire afternoon."

I too, was surprised. The time he had spent here just seemed to disappear. "How about if I fix us something to eat, then you can watch my favorite television show with me?"

"I should really go home and let you spend your evening as you like."

"Jonathan. I would like nothing better than to have you spend my evening with me."

"Are you sure?"

"Of course I'm sure. However, you have been fidgety ever since we started playing chess. Would you rather go home?"

He smiled. "No. Matter of fact I would rather stay, but at home I would have changed into some more comfortable clothing."

I happened to remember something, and it was something that I would enjoy myself. "Jonathan, I think I may be able to help you with that. Wait here. I'll be back in a moment."

I went into my bedroom, looked inside a box in the closet, pulled out what I was looking for, then undressed and put on my night gown and slippers. When I went back out to my kitchen, I said. "Jonathan. On the end of my bed is something you can change into that I think will suit your needs. You can leave the clothes you are wearing on a chair in my bedroom."

I had to grin when he looked at what I was wearing. He nodded at me, then went into my bedroom. When he came back, he was wearing the pajamas I had laid out for him on my bed. That and his socks.

We talked, but we were both just getting comfortable with the idea of wearing very little in each others company. I fixed us an omelet and after we had eaten we did the dishes together.

At eight O'clock I turned on the television and to the channel that shows my favorite documentaries. My couch is not large so we sat near each other. I'd fixed us some more tea and we were having cookies with the tea. As the show started, I just reached over and slipped my hand inside the pajama bottoms he was wearing. Jonathan didn't move or say anything as I slipped my hand around him. When he hardened, I pulled him out through the opening, and looked at his erection. "Jonathan. I haven't held one of these in such a long time."

"Marti. I haven't had one of these in a long time. I didn't even know if I could still get like this."

We both sat there like that for a few moments, then

I said. "Should we use it?"

He reached over and pulled the hem of my nightgown way up and as I opened my legs he put his hand down between my legs. As he rubbed me, he said. "I think we should try, and before it goes away."

We turned off the television, but left everything else as it was. In my bedroom I pulled off my nightgown and Jonathan took of the Pjs.

In bed I moved over and kissed him while I held onto his cock. He said. "Marti, lay down."

When I was on my back he moved up over me and wet the end of his cock, then slipped it into me, and said. "Oh, my goodness. You feel so good, Marti. So fucking good."

I don't know how long we screwed, but I came before Jonathan did. When he said. "Marti, I'm going to cum in you."

"Just do it, Jonathan. I've already cum. I just didn't want this to end."

Suddenly, Jonathan was shaking me awake. "Marti. Marti."

"Yes. What is it?"

"Someone's at your door."

I sat up, and realized it was morning already. "Oh my goodness. We slept clear through the night. That's probably my sister, Matti."

I got up out of bed and started for the door, but I stopped and looked back at Jonathan in bed. "She will want to come in. Will that be all right?"

He smiled as he said "Marti. It's your place. It's okay with me."

I went to the front door and opened it while I stood behind the door. Marti said. "What took you so long?"

As I closed the door she looked at me and then added. "And you're naked. What's going on?"

I knew she would find out so I just said. "Matti, keep your voice down. I have company."

"You have. . . .company?" She didn't wait for me. She simply went to my bedroom door and looked. "Oh my. You do have company."

There wasn't a lot I could do about things so I just said. "Jonathan, this is my sister, Matti."

"Good morning, Matti."

"Ohh, it could get better. Can I join you two in bed?"

I looked at Jonathan and he just shrugged his shoulders. As if to say it was my call. "I suppose you can."

She said. "Ill go to the bathroom and will be right back."

I crawled back in bed with Jonathan and moved my hand to take hold of him. I could feel him starting to stir as I kissed him. "I'm sorry if this bothers you?"

"It's not a problem for me, Matti."

"Jonathan. There is something else you should know about Matti. She likes to suck."

"Okay. What does she like. . . .oh my. You mean she likes to suck . . .?"

"Yes. It's what you're thinking."

His cock began to harden more as he thought about that happening.

Then, as Matti came around the end of my bed, he saw her breasts bouncing and swaying as she walked and his cock hardened even more.

As Matti got into bed with us, I moved my hand off of Jonathan's cock because I could see Matti's hand coming for him under the covers. When she had him in her hand, she said. "Ohh, that feels so good. I want it."

She pulled the covers down to his knees and moved down to his waist. As her lips slipped over him, he looked at me and mouthed.. "Oh fuck." Then his hand cupped my breast as she sucked him. He was facing me, but he wasn't seeing me. His mind was somewhere else. It was on the pleasure Matti was giving him by sucking on his cock.

After a few moments Matti raised up and moved up over Jonathan. Then she settled down on him as she guided him into her pussy. With her arms out straight her tits were almost touching his face. She moved her butt up and down as she fucked him, and Jonathan's hands went to her tits. As he took her nipples in his fingers I leaned over close to his ear and whispered. "When you think she is ready, pinch her nipples really hard. She likes it."

It didn't take long before he did just that. Matti groaned, then shuddered as she climaxed. She

nearly fell on Jonathan, but instead she moved off
him and said. "Marti. Finish him off for me. That
climax was so intense I can't do it for him."

I moved up over his cock and slipped down over
him. I fucked him hard and fast. He was spread
eagled on the bed. His legs open, his arms spread
out, but as he came in me he reached up around me
and pulled me down on him. As he pulled me
down tight to him, I came. After a few moments I
raised slightly and straightened one leg out, then
the other. Now I was lying flat on top of him. His
cock still in me.

MURIEL'S CONFESSION

I've known Jeffery since he was a kid. Actually I started baby sitting with him when he was three and I was twelve. It was never a problem spending time with him. That is until one day, when he was thirteen he was taking a shower and called out to me. "Muriel. I need a towel. Can you get me one?"

I found clean towels in a cupboard in the laundry and took him one. As I went into the bathroom, he was standing in the shower with the door open and holding out his hand for the towel. When I looked at him, it wasn't his eyes I looked at. Without thinking I said. "You are a big boy."

"Yeah and I will get bigger."

I didn't dare say a word, nor did he continue with what we were both thinking. I also found something else out that night as I stayed over because his folks were going to be gone for the whole weekend. Jeffery, is a peeping Tom. I always leave my bedroom door open slightly. It's a habit from years of baby sitting. It was a very warm night and I had the sheets pulled down to my waist. My left arm was lying up on my left hip and my tits were resting on the bed, one on top of the other. I thought I heard something, so I opened my eyes just enough to see, but not have them open all of the way.

I saw Jeffery looking in through the open part of the door and I knew he was looking at my tits.

After Jeffery was about nineteen, or so he would come over to my house to visit on occasion. He would also do things for me. Like cut my grass, or wash my car. Whatever he could to spend time with me. Late one Saturday morning I was sitting on my couch just finishing a cup of coffee, Wearing only a skimpy robe. When I saw him, walk up onto my porch. My front door was open though the screen was closed. This was to let the morning cool air circulate through the house.

I called out to him. "Come in Jeffery."

He came in and sat in a comfy chair that was at an angle to me, but where he could look at me as well. It was when he leaned over that I caught on that he was trying to look up between my legs. I pondered the idea for a bit. Do I get up and go put some clothes on, or what? Instead I scooted out to the edge of the couch, leaned back and pulled my robe open from top to bottom. His eyes bulged as he looked at me and he had to adjust his cock in his pants.

"Do you want this Jeffery?"

"Oh fuck yes."

I took him to my bedroom and I tried to lie still while he fucked me really slow and careful. But when I reached a climax from his cock, which I figured must be about two inches in diameter, and long enough to make most women want it in them, but my hips bucked up with the pleasure.

I had to reach up quickly with one hand to pull him down tight to my tits, and the other hand to reach down and hold his ass down so his cock was still in me.

"Don't stop now Jeffery."

"How long should I do this?"

"You'll know when to quit."

After he came in me, he asked. "Muriel, is it always this good?"

"Always."

I got married about a year later and my husband and I moved across town. The marriage lasted about five years, and as it happened I was in a store one afternoon when I met Jeffery's mother in the store. She asked me how things were with us, meaning myself and my husband. I told her I had gotten divorced about a year earlier. Two days later I picked up the phone as it rang. "Hello."

"Muriel. Ir's me. Jeffery."

"My goodness, how are you?"

"I'm good, but I'm calling to see if I can come see you. Say Friday evening?"

My feelings were mixed, but I said. "Okay. Sure, why not?"

When he came in, I closed the door behind him and said. "I was just going to the bathroom. Why don't you make yourself comfortable and I'll be right back."

"Can I get really comfy?"

I didn't think about what he had asked me. I just said. "Of course."

When I came back, I saw him sitting near the edge fo the couch. Naked. He was watching what I had on television so he didn't see me coming. His legs were open and I could see the end of his cock resting on the cushion, and this was when he was soft. I turned right back around and went into my bedroom to get undressed and to pull the covers and sheet way down. When I came back, I reached down to get the remote control and turned the set off. Then I reached for his hand and led him to my bed.

He fucked me for about three hours. Not continually, just time after time. After the second time I was sucking him up hard, but could not begin to get all of him in my mouth. I raised up off him and asked. "Jeffery, how long is this thing now?"

"I'm just a bit over eight inches long."

"Well come put this eight inches in me again."

I'm sixty-two now. My second husband has been gone for going on six years. About a year after he passed away, I called Jeffery, he knew why I called without asking the question. He comes by once a month, or so, and fortunately for me, he fucks me for about two hours each time. I love it.

NELLI & FRED

Fred and I are getting on in years. And with that comes a few problems that young people don't think about, well not much anyway. When you get older your sex drive, or the ability to fill your needs diminish to some extent. Maybe completely, though I'm not there yet. Fred's closer, in that he can get a hard on, but keeping it is the problem.

My pussy still gets wet when I can feel Fred's cock coming around in my hand, and I know he will do something to get me off, thank heavens for that. He still likes to suck on my tits, though they are not high and tight any longer, now they hang down, but he still likes them and handles them as though I'm thirty or something. His hands still roam all over my body, teasing me to a high heat and needing him to fuck me. Still, old age presents problems.

However, recently he came up with a solution that has worked out quite well for us, especially me. He found a place where he could order a hollow strap on cock. You have to measure yourself when you cock is hard so you can order one that your cock will fit inside of when you have a hard on.

Now, when I need a fuck, Fred puts on his strap on cock with his cock inside, then reaches down and opens my pussy with his fingers and slips that nice hard cock into my waiting and wanting pussy. At first it seems odd, but you get used to it. It's like fucking a man wearing a condom. But it's Fred on top of me and he fucks me as long as I want him too. He can fuck me hard, or slow and gentle and he doesn't get off too soon.

MARION

Yesterday we had driven most of the day, but we arrived just in time for dinner. I'm not sure how Marion, my mother-in-law knows how to time our arrival like she does, but she does and she had dinner waiting for us. Susan and I had driven to my in-laws intending on spending a week with them on our vacation. During dinner, Frank, my father-in-law, asked. "Joe, I'd planned on going fishing tomorrow. Would you two like to come along?"

I knew he knew that I'm not a fisherman, but I knew Susan wanted to spend some quality time with her dad, so, I said. "I think I'll pass on that, but Susy might want to go."

She looked at me and said. "You don't mind?"

"Not at all. Enjoy yourself."

"What are you going to do all day?"

"Not much. Lay around mostly. Unless I get on Marion's nerves."

Marion said. "You're not going to be in my way. I have nothing going on tomorrow."

Now, this morning, Susan got up about six thirty to get ready to go with her dad. She asked, "Anything I can do for you when we get home? Can I get you something on the way home, or?"

"How about making love tonight?"

"Oh. I think I'll be much too tired for that."

"Yeah. I imagine you will be." Susan and I fuck about four times a year. I know, that's a terrible rate of sexual intimacy, but what am I going to do. When I had asked about her parents, she had told me that they 'do it' around twelve times a year. Crap, that's not good either.

I lay in bed alone for a bit and played with my cock. I thought about jacking off, but I didn't. I got up about eight o'clock, pulled on a Tee shirt and my boxer shorts, then having heard Marion puttering around in the kitchen, I headed that way. The bedroom door opened easily and quietly. As I came into the kitchen, I surprised Marion as she was just sitting down at the far end of her table with a cup of coffee in her hands. Her morning robe buttoned all the way up to the top. She looked up at my eyes as I came in, but then hers dropped right back down to my shorts. She asked, still looking at my crotch. "I didn't know you were up yet. Can I get you some coffee?"

"Nah. I'll get it." After I poured myself some coffee, I turned toward and leaned back against the counter top facing her. I said. "How much time do we have to play today?"

She looked up at me, and said. "To play. What. . ."

I interrupted her by saying. "They left about, what, seven, or so?"

"Yes, just shortly after that."

"How long will it take them to get out to the bay?"

"Hour and a half, give or take."

"Then what happens?"

"They will need to get the boat unloaded, and ready to go offshore. That'll be about an hour. Frank will wait for slack water so they can go out with the first part of the ebb tide. Then, they'll fish until the slack water just before a flood tide, and ride that calm water back into the harbor. An hour and a half later, they will just about be home."

I was doing the math in my head, and when I had it figured out, I said. "So. They won't be home much before seven or so tonight?"

"Probably."

"Good. That gives us, what? About ten, or eleven hours to play?"

"You said play?"

"Yes. I thought we might spend the day fucking?"

She put her cup down, and said. "You're not serious?"

I put my cup on the counter, then walked to the chair at the other end of the table, pulled off my Tee shirt, then pulled my shorts down and off. I put them on the chair at that end of the table, and walked back to where she sat. I stood in front of her, my hard cock standing straight out in front of her face, and I said. "Does this look like I'm serious?"

"Ohh, my God."

I wanted to be sure she was okay with me doing this, so I leaned over, took her face in my hands kissed her gently and asked. "Are you afraid of me?"

"No, Joe. I'm not afraid, it's just . . . "

I leaned over further and kissed her with more passion. I felt her hands come up, one cupping my balls, the other circling around my cock. When she felt my hardness, her tongue found mine and when I heard her go. "Umm." I was sure she was hungry for a cock.

I stood up and pulled her up from her chair. Then I leaned over and started opening the buttons of her robe from the bottom up. After I finished all of the buttons, I slipped the robe off her shoulders and put it on the chair behind her. I pulled at her hand and moved back over to the counter. As I leaned back, with my legs together, I told her. "Come close to me, and put your arms up around my neck.

She moved close to me, but said. "I can't get any closer."

"Yes you can. Open your legs and straddle me."

As she came to me with her legs apart, her arms went up over my shoulders and around my neck, my cock was pressed against her lower tummy. I reached down and pushed it down between her legs, then put my hands on the cheeks of her ass and pulled her tight to me. She laid her head against my neck, and said. "Oh, God, Joe. We shouldn't do this."

"Listen, you're a hungry woman and I'm a fucking hungry man. Okay?"

I felt her head nod yes against me, so I said. "Lets go to bed in your guest bedroom. Pull the covers down, and you get your ass on the bed with your legs open. Okay?"

Softly I heard. "Okay."

I let her go and watched her ass undulating as she walked in front of me. In the bedroom she got up on the bed like I asked. When I was on my knees, but had not lowered myself down onto her,

I started to reach my fingers to my mouth, when she said. "You won't need that?"

"I won't?"

"No."

I leaned over, but before I could reach down to open her, she beat me to it. Her fingers pulled her open, and then she guided me inside her pussy. I took two strokes, then lay still a moment. I said. "Lets fuck like animals this first time, then we can take longer the next few times."

"How many times, are we going to fuck?"

"As many as we can."

"Okay, fuck me like an animal who needs my pussy really badly."

I don't think we lasted ten minutes the first time. The second time was longer, but still not enough. We dozed for a bit, then when I woke I pulled her right leg up over my hip, then her left leg between my legs, and I reached over to open her and pushed my cock into her pussy. Yes, she was awake. We fucked like that slowly but only for a little while. I had to get on top of her to give her a good fuck. After I got on top of her, we fucked for quite awhile this time.

More to feel each other and to just enjoy being together in bed. After we got off this time, we got up and made a late breakfast together. Naked all the time.

After breakfast, she said. "I have a soap opera coming on. One that I watch every day. Do you mind?"

"Not at all." I went with her to her living room and we sat on the couch to watch her television program. Not being a follower of soaps, I reached down between her legs to rub her clit. She put her hand on top of mine to stop me because I drew her attention away from the television. I finally reached down and started playing with my cock. It happened as I wagged it at her that she turned off the television, moved slightly away from me, then leaned over and kissed the head of my cock. Then she got up and straddled me on the couch. With her tits in my face, she slipped down over my shaft and began fucking me. She got off, but stayed with me until she brought me up to a climax as well.

We showered after that and she had told me she had to go to the store to get some stew meat for dinner and wanted me to come with her. I said. "Yes. I'll come along if you don't wear any panties under your dress."

"Oh, God, Joe. I don't go anywhere without my underwear on."

"Do this today. I think you'll enjoy being naked under your dress while you are out in public."

As we walked around the market getting the stuff she wanted, she said to me. "Joe, this makes me . . . Horny. . . You know. Without having panties on I almost want someone to look up my skirt to see me."

"The idea of being naked like this does this to most people. I'll drive home and while we are in the car you can pull your dress up to expose yourself to me, or anyone who might happen to look inside the car as we are moving through traffic."

She hadn't responded to that comment, but she gave me the car keys as we left the store. It didn't take long until she leaned the passenger seat back some, and pulled her dress up to her waist. Then she opened her legs. She asked. "Do you have women do this all of the time when they ride with you?"

"No. But I have found that many women like to expose themselves in cars. Most of them show off their tits while they drive, or travel in a car."

After we got home Marion asked me to fix the vegetables for the stew, while she got the meat ready. I followed her instructions, then satisfied, she said. "Okay. You can do as you like now and I'll finish getting this started in the crock pot."

I went into my bedroom, took my clothes off, then went to the bathroom. By the time I got back to the kitchen, Marion was washing her hands in the kitchen sink. When I walked up behind her, she had reached for the towel to dry her hands. I reached down and lifted the hem of her dress up over her waist and started rubbing my cock across the cheeks of her ass. She finished drying her hands, then moved me backwards a bit and turned around and walked over to the table. She pulled her dress up well above her waist, then leaned way over on top of the table.

As she spread her legs slightly apart, she said.
"Can you see my pussy?"

"Yes."

"Fuck it."

I moved up behind her, bent over slightly as I wet
the head of my cock with my fingers and saliva
from my mouth, then I pushed into her from
behind. Holding her hips with my hands, we
fucked like that for several minutes. Shortly,
Marion said. "Joe, I'm going to cum. . . . Joe, I'm
cumming right now, . . . uuh. . . uhh. . .uhh. .
.Ohhh fuck. . . Oh God that' was good."

I said. "Marion. I'm going to cum in your pussy. . .
now." And I shoved as deep into her as I could get.

We went to her bathroom to clean up, then
knowing the day was over for this kind of playing,
we settled down at the kitchen table to talk, and
wait for Frank and Susan to get home.

After dinner, everyone watched television for
awhile, then Susan said. "I'm beat. I need to go to
bed."

She slept all night, but in the morning, as I lay
awake and was listening to Marion putter around
the kitchen, my cock got hard thinking about her

and fucking her. I felt Susan stir, then when she opened her eyes, she reached over for me. She found my cock hard, and said. "I had a talk with my dad yesterday."

"Okay. So?"

"I told him how much sex we have a year, and he said I should take better care of you."

Before I could respond, she pulled the covers down off me, and scooted down on the bed. As she sucked my cock, I noticed the noise in the kitchen had stopped, but didn't pay any attention to it, as I was watching Susan's mouth going up and down on my cock. I was close to a climax when I happened to look toward the door. Marion had apparently come to tell us breakfast was almost ready, but she was standing partway in the doorway, her hand inside her robe rubbing herself while she watched Susan sucking me off. With the excitement of having my cock sucked, and being watched by Marion, I came in Susan's mouth. When my vision cleared, I looked back at the door, but it had been pulled nearly closed, and Marion was gone. Susan's head was lying on my leg, my cock still in her mouth. She made sure I was as dry as she could get me, then lifted up and said. "We should get up now."

ODD

Glenn, and I have been friends with benefits for some time now. Usually we just fuck in the normal manner, but the last time he was here I asked him before he left if the next time he would do something odd to me. So, today, when he came over, he did indeed do things differently. This is how it went today after I opened the door and let him in.

He pulled my mouth to his and kissed me hard, then said. "Take your fucking clothes off. . . .now. Right fucking now."

I got undressed right where we stood, then he pulled me by my nipple to my bathroom doorway, then said. "Reach up over your head and hold onto the door trim up there over your head and don't let go until I tell you, you can."

"Are you kidding?"

He reached down and smacked me hard on the ass. "No. I'm not kidding."

As I stood there, he moved over to my bed and got undressed while I watched.

"How long do I have to stand here, Glenn?"

He came over to me, then smacked me on the ass again, and said. "Until I tell you to let go."

He squeezed past me and went into my bathroom. I kept my hands up on the door trim, but I turned to watch what he was doing. He went over to the toilet and peed. Then he turned to look at me and started stroking his cock. He went back by me and into my bedroom, then said.

"Where's your fuck toy?"

I knew what he meant, so I said. "It's in the top drawer of my dresser. On the left side under my socks."

After he found my dildo, he came back to me and said. "Open your legs."

I spread them, but strained to keep my fingers touching the top of the door frame. Glenn, reached in between my legs and opened my pussy, then eased my dildo up into me.

"Close your legs and keep that fucking toy clamped in your pussy."

He moved back over to my bed and got on top, then got up onto his elbows and knees. Then he said. "Look at how I'm positioned on the bed. Do you see how I am with my ass close to the bed?"

"Yes. I can see."

"I want you to reach down and hold that fuck toy in your pussy. Then come over here and get up on the bed and get in the same position. But, don't let your toy come out of your pussy. When you have it, right, you can let go of the toy, but you should be low enough so that it will be resting on the bed and stay in your pussy."

It wasn't too easy, but I did as he said. "Now what, Glenn?"

He came over to me, reached for my hair with his hand, and turned my head toward him. Then, he fucked me in the mouth. Just fucked me in the mouth until he'd had enough. When he was done, he said. "Stay there just like that."

I stayed where I was and watched him getting dressed. Then he said. "You wait just like that for three minutes after I leave."

After he left, I watched the clock. When my time was up, I rolled over on the bed and fucked my pussy hard with that fuck toy.

OLDER

Believe it or not, I met Katherine through an internet connection. She was looking for someone to look after her needs. It seems old age often has no sway on the mental yearning. I was apprehensive at first, but after meeting her, I no longer had any doubts.

Our first meeting took place at her place, and when I arrived she met me at the door. As it opened, I said. "HI. I'm Howard."

She smiled at me, and answered. "Howard, I'm Kathy. Please come in."

We had tea together and talked about a good many things. All of it was to get comfortable with each other. To develop a feeling of mutual trust, and it was to be expected. I have not done much of this kind of thing, and I am certain she hasn't. Near the end of our time together, and we both knew it was time to part company. I asked. "So, Katherine, do you want to get together again?"

She returned my smile. "Yes. I think so. Only next time perhaps we can enjoy each other in much closer company."

"You mean physically?"

"Yes."

"Okay. Send me a note when you want me."

"Howard. I want you now, But, for the moment
can we plan on an afternoon this next week. About
this time?"

."That sounds good to me. I'll come by unless you
send me a note and tell me not to come."

It was Thursday before I got to her house again,
and I hoped I wasn't too late. I knocked at her door
and waited. It seemed some time but soon I heard
the safety chain on the inside of her door come
loose and drop. I knew then she had looked
through her peephole in the door to see who was
here. She was smiling as she opened the door. I
was surprised as she was only wearing a robe.

"Howard, come in, I was just about to go take a
nap."

"I can come back another time?"

"No. No, please." As she stepped aside, I walked
into her living room.

I had a thought. "Why don't you go ahead and get
into bed to take your nap?"

"Really?"

"Sure, then if you don't mind, I'll climb in with you. I'll stay until you drift off then I'll leave and lock your door behind me."

She smiled, "You are a wicked man, Howard."

She took my hand and led me to her bedroom and I watched as she took her robe off and laid it on a large quilt box at the end of her bed. I was pleased to see she still has a decent body. Even for her age she is in pretty good shape. After she got into bed, I sat on a chair near the head of her bed and took off my shoes and socks. Then I took them around to the other side of the bed. Back in front of her I took my shirt off and laid it on the quilt box with her robe. Again, in front of her I stood close to the bed and undid my belt buckle, then the top button of my pants. After I pulled the zipper down, I slid my pants and my shorts down over my hips, then down so I could step out of them. With my pants off I stood close to the bed and her hand came out to hold me. She said.

"Howard, it has been so very long since I've even seen a naked man, let alone hold onto his penis."

I let her play with my cock, and it hardened, and as it did she grinned like a woman in heat who was about to get what she wanted. I pulled away from her and went around to the other side of the bed and got in bed with her. I moved over close and her other hand found me quickly.

I leaned over, pulling the covers down, and began to suck her nipples. I could feel her tugging at my cock, so I said. "Katherine?"

"Yes?"

"Do you want me to fuck you?"

"Howard, you talk nasty."

"Aahh, so you'd rather I said. Katherine, my dear, would you like to fornicate?"

She was still for a moment, then said. "I see what you mean."

"And so?"

"Yes. I'd like you to . . . I'd like you to fuck me."

"Okay. So here's what I'm going to do. I'm going to suck on your nipples a bit longer. While I'm doing that I'm going to play with your pussy with my hand, then I'm going to mount you and fuck you."

"Oh, lordy. I like the sounds of that."

As my head came back to her tits I could feel her
other hand reach up to hold me there. My cock was
still hard in her other hand. And, as I reached down
for her, she opened her legs wide. I hadn't rubbed
her clit but for a few moments when she was very
wet. I let her nipple slip from my mouth, and
moved up over her. In between her legs I reached
down to open her pussy. When I started to push
into her, I realize it was not going to be a quick
entry, she has not had a cock in a long time and her
pussy was very tight. So, inch by inch I eased into
her. When I was all the way in, I asked, "You
okay?"

"Howard, I am very fucking okay. Just fuck me
now."

I took my time, even then it must have felt damn
good to her because she came much sooner than I
had expected. As I started to fuck her for my own
pleasure, she said. "Ohh God that's so good."

When I came in her, she almost growled as she
said. "Oh damn that is a fucking good cock you
have there. Oh fuck yes. Howard I'd like you to
fuck me often. Okay? I want you to fuck me a lot."

It was a Friday afternoon when I went to see
Katherine again, and she was waiting for me. She

knew I was coming and I think she had been watching for me. When I got to her door, she opened it right away. When I got inside, she was only wearing her bathrobe. As she came to me, I pulled the sash open and then opened her robe. Then I reached out for her nipples and pulled her to me and kissed her with a fiery passion. Her hands shot out around me and she pulled tight to me. When our lips parted, she said. "Oh my God, Howard. You make me so. . . .horny."

"Just kissing you makes you horny?"

"Well sometimes, but no. Pulling my tits to get me to you. That's what got to me. No body has ever done that to me before."

"What else makes you horny?"

"Well, lately, lots of things."

"For instance?"

She smiled, as if she was going to reveal a real secret to me. "This week I've been looking at some of those places on the internet. You know the ones where they show men and women doing things. I'm surprised at how many women suck on a man's pen. . . .ah. . . cock."

"Most women enjoy oral sex."

"I also saw men with their heads buried between a woman's legs. Do men like doing that as well."

"Of course they do."

"Why?"

"Why. It simple isn't it. It gives pleasure to the partner. That's why."

"Have you ever done that to a woman?"

"Of course."

She was still a moment. I'd eased off her nipples but was still holding her tits in my hands. Then she said. "I think I might like to try that stuff sometime."

I dropped her tits, took her hand and pulled her toward her bedroom. "Come on. Get your robe off and lie on top of your bed. Move up high so I have room to get on the bed below you."

She didn't say anything, but she did as I asked. I put a pillow under her ass, then I got undressed while she watched me. Then I moved in between her legs. I had to part her muff, and we'd be cutting that shorter soon. I started by kissing her inner thighs but didn't waste much time there. I got right to work on her clit. She was responsive to the point that I think it even surprised her. Her hands were rubbing her nipples and she began to talk in hushed tones. I knew her climax was climbing up from the very bottom of her feet. When she came, it was with a loud moaning noise coming from deep within her. Her convulsions from the climax were heavy. After she'd climaxed, I got up off the bed and pulled the pillow out from under her ass and then I got hold of her ankles and pulled her down farther on the bed. She hardly moved as I got in between her legs, opened her pussy with my fingers and pushed my cock in her. I fucked her hard and fast.

As I lay beside her, she came over to me. Pushing her tits hard to me as she reached her left arm over me and her left leg slid up over mine. We both dozed off and when I woke she was holding onto my cock. I reached over and kissed her on the forehead.

She looked up at me and said. "Howie, that was wonderful. And the way you fucked me for yourself afterwards was good too."

"I'm glad you liked it."

"And, Howie. I think next time I'd like to try sucking you."

PANTS

Jimmy had come to see me, and he often does. He comes by to see if I need anything. Perhaps a ride to the store, to get to a doctor's appointment, and things like that. In reality, Jimmy likes me. He's found out that I rise late in the mornings and out of habit I wash my dishes from the night before while I'm still wearing my nightgown. It is thin material and I know my nipples show when they rub against the material as I move around.

When Jimmy came by yesterday morning I was just getting started on my dishes and saw him drive in my driveway. I dried my hands and went to the door to let him in. He followed me into the kitchen and leaned against the counter so we could talk while I did my dishes. Of course Jimmy was not always looking at my eyes as we talked, but I don't mind him watching my nipples as they move around. Some times I can see the bulge in his pants when he looks at me, and I like that too. Yesterday was no exception.

I said. "I'm just about finished her, why don't you go sit at the table and I'll fix you an iced tea."

He sat with his chair pulled out from the table so he could still see me, and I figured this is what he would do. I had a plan and was about to use it. I dried my hands on a hand towel, then reached up

into the cupboard for a glass knowing full well
Jimmy was hoping to see my ass as I stretched up
to reach the shelf for the glass. He didn't quite get
what he wanted, but close to it as I tried to fulfill
his desire, but my nightgown just didn't raise high
enough.

I went to the refrigerator and poured the iced tea
into the glass, but not much more than half way.
As I walked toward Jimmy, I pretended to have a
coughing spell, and I dumped the iced tea right in
Jimmy's lap. Perfectly I might add. He jumped up
saying. "Oh my God, that's cold."

"Oh, Jimmy. I'm so sorry."

"Shelly, I'm a mess."

"Yes, you are. Tell you what. Take your pants off
and I'll put them in the washing machine. It won't
take long to wash and dry them, and you'll be good
as new."

"Ahh, but what will I wear until then?"

"Nothing. You can go sit on my couch while I get
your pants going."

"But, I'll be naked from the waist down."

"Jimmy, I know what men look like."

"Okay, I guess." It was fun watching him take his pants off. He tried to hide his hard cock, but that was nearly impossible as he stepped out of his pants. He turned away from me quickly but I still had a nice view of him.

After I'd put his pants into the wash, I joined him on the couch. I sat right next to him and looked down at his cock. Though it had softened to some degree, it still looked good to me. I reached over and slid my fingers up and down its length a few times, and as it grew hard, I said. "It's been a while since I've seen one of these."

I knew from his groan that he really liked my hand touching his cock. I reached down and pulled the hem of my night gown up to reveal my pussy, and then took hold of his hand and laid it inside my thigh and then I patted my mound. "Maybe we should see if it fits in here?"

I stood and took his hand and as he stood his cock was straight out in front of him. I could have pulled him like a pull toy. I led him to my bedroom and pulled my nightgown up over my head while he finished getting undressed. I lay on my back with my legs' wide open and as he moved up over me I reached down to guide him into my waiting wet. He took his time fucking me and made sure I came first, then he fucked me hard and fast. He's as noisy as I am when he cums.

We were laying there when I heard the washing machine stop, so I got up and went to put his pants in the dryer. When I came back, I moved up on the bed a bit higher and had him move down some, saying. "Play with my tits and suck on them while you pants are drying."

The dryer was still going when Jimmy decided to fuck me again.

POSING

I'm involved with a man that some would consider. . . .different. But that's one of the reasons I like him so much. He's the kind of guy that will take you out to the edge of your comfort zone. A sexual daring you might say. Let me tell you about something he did with me recently. My place has a deck out in the front that overlooks a large popular meadowland. I also have steps that lead down from my deck to the area below my place. Many people frequent the paths that lead into and out of the trees and different areas of the meadow, so foot traffic around here is sporadic.

When Charlie got here, and inside, he took me in his arms and pulled me close to him as the robe I was wearing fell open to reveal my nude body, then his tongue searched for mine as we kissed. He treats me well with his tongue, if you know what I mean. He had something planned for me, and all I knew was that it involved taking pictures of me. Yes, pictures. You know the ones they call 'action' pictures. Well, that kind of picture is what he wanted to take. And, we were going to use my camera.

When our lips parted, he asked. "Are you ready?"

"Yes."

"Okay. Get your camera and I'll meet you by your sliding door leading out to your deck."

When I got to the door I started to hand him the camera, but he said. "Turn around."

I turned so my back was to him, and his hands came around under my arms and he cupped my tits in his hands. "Okay. Show me how your camera works."

"Charlie. You have me exposed to anyone who might come along on one of the paths down below."

"Yes I do. Show me how the camera works."

After I explained it to him, we went outside, and he had me lean up against the deck railing, but facing the house. "I want you to pull your robe down off your shoulders, but keep it closed under your tits."

I did what I though he wanted, and asked. "Is this the way you want me?"

"Yes. That's good. I just want a tit picture of you in this photo. If you let your robe fall open I'll be trying to look down between your legs."

After he took that picture, he had me turn around facing out away from the house. He went down about four or five steps, then turned to me and said. Put your arms on the deck railing and lean out over the edge.

What I want you to do is shake your tits loose out over the edge so they are hanging down from you."

Oh fuck. He wanted my tits exposed to the open area in front of me. "Charlie. Someone might see me."

"Cary. Just fucking does it."

I was nervous but I posed the way he wanted me too. Then he had me come down the steps to where he was standing and he explained what he wanted next. He stood close to me as I left my left foot where it was, but moved my right foot up three steps. I had to stretch to do it, but I did it the way he wanted me too. When he sat down on one of the steps, I began to wonder about this next picture.

"Turn slightly toward me." I turned.

"Okay let the right side of your robe fall open." I let it go and it fell down to the steps.

He took the left edge of my robe and pulled it up to my hip. "Hold this right here."

With my left hand holding my robe up on my hip, I was fully exposed to him. He moved closer to me and when he leaned over I knew he was going to take a picture of my pussy being stretched open by my legs being so far apart.

He took two pictures of me this way, then he began to rub one of my inner thighs, but he did not touch my pussy. Then he rubbed the other one. Fuck I wanted to feel his fingers on me and he was only teasing me.

 "What do you call this lovely thing here between your legs?"

"When you first got here, it was my pussy. Now it's a fucking cunt and you better damns well touch it while you are there."

"Are you enjoying being out here with me taking pictures of you like this?"

I would never have done this kind of thing, but for some reason Charlie really knows how to get my juices flowing. "Fuck yes. I like it. It makes me feel like a fucking slut though." When his fingers tugged at my lips, I felt it clear through my body. Fuck I wanted his cock.

"One more pose out here. Go up to the top step, then squat down and let your robe come open and your legs come apart so I can see you."

He took a picture looking up under me. And said. "That is a beautiful fucking cunt to look at. Lets go in the house for some more pictures of the slut I'm with."

In the house he said. "While I get undressed I'd like you to take your robe off. Then meet me on the small sofa you have in your dressing room."

I suspected what he might like so when he got to me I was leaning back but with my ass sitting near the edge of the seat. My legs were wide open. He knelt down in front of me and took a picture of me seated this way. "That's a good fucking picture."

He got up and moved next to me, but with some room between us. Then he put his left foot up on my sofa. This left his right foot on the floor and of course his cock and balls right there for the offering.

"So, what would a slutty woman do right now?"

I leaned over and took his cock into my mouth. He began to tell me what he wanted next as I sucked on him. He pulled his cock out of my mouth. "Lets get you into bed."

He arranged me for a picture that left my left arm lying on top of the sheet he had covered my hips with. My right hand was up covering my eyes, as if to block out the light so I could sleep. Then he picked my tits up by the nipples and arranged them for the next picture. With this done, he said. "Okay, one more."

He had me get into the middle of the bed, and on my back. The sheets pulled off me, and he had me help him put a pillow under my hips, which of course raised my cunt up slightly. With my knees raised and my legs wide open he took another picture of my cunt. As he moved up to put the camera on my night stand, he said. "Stay that way."

I felt him move up onto the bed as he got between my legs. Then he started kissing me on my inner thighs. Slowly, one side, then the other. When his mouth moved over the lips of my cunt, I fucking near came. He licked me with a passion and when I got close I told him. "I'm going to come. Oh fuck yes. Now, right fucking . . . . noowww. '

He licked me a few moments more, then moved to where my left leg was between his legs and my right leg was up over his hip. Then as we talked he eased his cock into my very hot and waiting cunt.

TABLES & CHAIRS

God this man does things to me that make me horny. Even later when I think about what took place. Like earlier today. It almost always happens that when he comes to me, we start out doing something sexually. Often without even saying a word to each other. I mean it only takes a kiss.

I met him at the door wearing only an open robe. We did talk today before he started with me. But, briefly. We kissed right away. His tongue searching for mine and his hands found their way inside my robe and down onto the cheeks of my ass. I thought about other places his tongue searches on me. Right away he led me to my dining room and then he pulled a chair out from the table and said. "Sit up here."

I sat on the edge of the table, and watched him undoing his belt, then the top button of his pants, then the zipper. He pulled his pants off and dropped them on his shoes that he had taken off first. He sat on the chair and leaned over to me. I put my feet on the edges of the chair and spread my legs as wide as I could. I knew fucking well he was going to taste me. You know, eat my pussy. I leaned back on my elbows and let him lick my clit. Almost to the point I climaxed, but not quite.

He moved away from me, and said. "Get your fucking cunt down off the table and sit here." He pointed down to his cock.

I slipped off the table and straddled him, then eased down onto his waiting shaft. Then I fucked him. My tits were bouncing in his face as I kept up my rhythm and felt my need searching for a way to its release. Awkward, maybe. But you never pay any attention to that at the time. You just want to get off.

THE BABY SITTER

Mom told me last night that she and dad were going to be gone for the whole weekend, and that she was going to have, Chrissy, from down the street come stay with me while they were gone. I told her I was twelve and didn't need a baby sitter. She told me she was having Chrissy come stay anyway and that she would fix my meals and see that I didn't stay up half the night watching television. Chrissy is sixteen and a fox, and I like her so I told mom that it would be okay.

So, when she got here a little bit ago, I said hello to her, then went back to watching a show on the television. I was really listening to mom's conversation with Chrissy, but they didn't know I was paying any attention to them.

"He needs to take a shower and should be in bed by ten thirty. Also there is a night light in his room because he used to have bad dreams and the light seems to help. There's plenty of food in the cupboards and refrigerator, but Tim's not a picky eater."

"Okay. And, I'm to sleep in your guy's bed?"

"Yes. Is that okay?"

"Sure."

Later, a couple of hours after mom and dad left, Chrissy was fixing us something to eat, she asked. "What time do you usually take your shower?"

"Just before I go to bed."

"Most of the time that's when I take mine too."

I smiled at her and said. "Just before I go to bed?"

She smiled back. "No, silly. Just before I go to bed."

I was watching television when Chrissy said. "Why don't you take your shower early, then you can sit around to watch something on television with me?"

I looked at the clock and it was only eight o'clock. "You mean now?"

"Sure. Why not?"

I couldn't think of any reason not to, so I said. "Okay."

I went to my bedroom and got undressed except for my shorts, then headed for the bathroom. Chrissy was coming out of the bathroom with all of the towels.

"Your mom said we can use fresh towels, so I'll get one for you. But first I want to do something else."

"Okay." I went in the bathroom and got into the glass walled shower. While I was in there washing, Chrissy came in. She had a towel in her hands, but she just stood there looking at me. I couldn't hide behind clear glass doors, so I could only let her look.

"Tim. You're kinda big for being only twelve."

"I think I'm average height?"

"I don't mean tall."

I knew what she meant then, because she was looking down. I started to get longer as she watched. "I need my towel."

"Oh. Yeah." She handed it to me, then left the bathroom.

When I came out of the bathroom, Chrissy was coming out of my bedroom. I thought she had something in her hand. But, she said. "Do you have pajama's to wear?"

"No. I don't sleep in anything."

"I've got an extra big Tee shirt you can wear while we watch TV. I'll get it for you."

She brought it to me in my bedroom, then said. "Okay. I'll go get my shower now."

I was sitting on the floor leaning against the couch watching television, when I heard Chrissy call me. "Tim. I forgot to get a fresh towel for myself. Will you get me one?"

I got one from the closet where mom puts them, and took it to Chrissy in the bathroom. When I got in there, she was standing in the shower waiting for me. Boy, does he have big boobs. Bigger than mom's. I think. I wanted to stay in there and watch her dry off, but I was growing again and poking out, so I left to back to the living room.

When Chrissy came in the living room with me, she sat on the couch near me. But she raised her left foot and over my head and put it on the couch behind me, the other one was on the floor near me. I turned to look at her and I could see up under her Tee shirt. I've never seen one of those before, so it was hard not to look. A minute or so later, when I tried to sneak a peek I happen to look up first. Chrissy smiled at me as our eyes met.

"You like looking at my pussy?"

"I'm sorry, Chrissy. I couldn't help it."

"Tell you what. Let me stand up a moment."

I moved over a bit and she swung her left leg up over my head and stood up, then she took her Tee shirt off and laid it on the couch, then she sat back down like she had been before. With her legs open, but now I could really see her.

"Go ahead and look all you want."

I turned around on the floor and looked right at her between the legs. While I was looking, I grew long, but I didn't care now. "Your hair is short?"."

"Yeah. I cut it often."

"You do. Why cut it?"

She reached down with her hand and began to rub herself. "So I can do this and not have a lot of hair in the way." While she rubbed, she pulled herself open and I could see up inside of her a little ways. I wanted to reach down and play with myself, but didn't.

"Maybe we should go to bed early, too?"

"Okay." I knew that if we went to bed now I could play with myself while I thought about how she looked between her legs. I went into my bedroom, got into bed and reached up to turn my light off. When I did, it got really dark. I turned my light back on and found out my night light was gone. I remembered Chrissy had, had something in her hand when she left my room earlier, so I got up and even though I was naked, I went to ask her.

The door to my parent's bedroom was open and Chrissy was lying under the covers, but the lamp on the night stand next to the bed was still on. "Chrissy, did you take my night light?"

"Oh, yeah. I borrowed it. I don't like to sleep in a completely dark room."

"Me neither."

"We could share it?"

"How?"

"You could sleep in here with me."

There wasn't any thing to think about. To sleep with Chrissy, wow. "Okay. I can do that."

I was in bed with her for a few short minutes when I took a chance and said. "Chrissy, I'm cold."

She turned up on her side to face me, then stretched out her left arm and said. "Come cuddle up to me. I'll get you warm."

I moved over next to her. My right arm was down between us and I could feel her upper leg with my hand. My left arm was up between us and my hand was on her boob. Her nipple was between my fingers. I thought nipples were soft, but Chrissy's was hard. I got long and hard almost right away. She said. "Tim, you're poking me."

"Chrissy, I can't help it."

"Okay, I'll hold you so you don't poke me there."

She wrapped her hand around me, then after a few moments she began to move it back and forth. Kinda like I do when I play with myself. It didn't take long and I had to say. "Chrissy. If you keep doing that, I'm gonna squirt on you."

"Will you?"

"Yes, and I squirt a lot."

"When you say 'squirt' you mean, ' you cum, or your cumming. . . .Turn over on your back."

When I was on my back, Chrissy reached up to get a tissue from the box on the night stand next to the bed. Then she turned back to me and gave me the tissue and said. "Just before you cum, you tell me. Then you can catch it with the tissue."

Then she reached over and began to play with my prick. It didn't take long, and I had to say. "Chrissy, I'm gonna cum now."

After I finished, I said. "I need another tissue, okay?"

She handed me another one and said. "You really do cum a lot."

After we laid there a few more seconds, she turned over on her back and said. "Put your hand between my legs and open them."

I moved over closer and rubbed my hand down her tummy, then over her hairy part, then down between her legs. I was kinda surprised when my hand got kinda wet as I moved down between her legs. Then I pushed her right leg over toward the other edge of the bed, and then pulled the other one toward me. "How's that?"

"That's good. Now get between my legs and when your ready move up and push your prick into my pussy."

"Do I get to a . . . fuck you Chrissy?"

"Fuck yes, you're gonna fuck me. And, more than once."

I couldn't believe how good it felt to push my prick into Chrissy's pussy. But before I started fucking her, she said. "Tim. Fuck me slow. I'll tell you when you can go fast, Okay?"

"Okay." When I started fucking, Chrissy, I was going slow, but she put her hands up on my butt and I could feel her fingers signaling me when to push into her, and when to pull out. After a few minutes I could hear her making sounds, like. "Uh. . .uh. . .uh." Then she pulled my butt down hard against her and she wiggled under me. I was surprised when her hands fell off of me, and she said. "Okay, Tim. Fuck me hard and fast now. I did and I could tell soon enough to warn her.

"Chrissy, I'm gonna cum now." And I jammed my prick into her. I think she wiggled under me again.

After we fucked again in the morning, before we got up, she said. "After we have lunch, I'll teach you something new."

We didn't even get dressed, and at lunch time she fixed us both sandwiches. When we finished eating, she said. "Move your chair back away from the table a little bit."

When I was where she wanted me, she got up on the table and swivelled around in front of me. Then she put her feet up on my knees and made me open my legs, which also opened her legs. She leaned back on her left elbow and with her other hand she said. "Do you see that little pink bump right there?"

I looked to where she was pointing at a shiney pink kinda button at the top of her pussy. "Yeah. I see it."

"Lick me there."

I leaned over and licked her little pink button and heard her kinda moan. Then I lifted my head and asked. "Does that feel good?"

"That feels very fucking good. Here, lets trade places and I'll show you what I mean."

When I was sitting on the table with my feet on her knees, she leaned over and put her mouth on my prick. I could only say. "Oh. . oh. . .yes. That does feel good."

Chrissy said. "Okay. Lets go fuck in your bed."

"My bed?"

"Yes. It has to look like you've spent some time in it."

When we got to my bedroom, I saw she had put my night light back. "You get on the bottom, Tim."

"Me, on the bottom?"

"Yes. I gonna fuck you this time."

It was odd being on the bottom and being fucked by a girl, but I liked it.

We fucked two more times before my folks came home on Sunday afternoon. Just before Chrissy was ready to leave my mom asked her.

"Can you do this again a month from now?"

Chrissy looked at me and I nodded enthusiastically. She said. "Sure. Anytime."

THE BUTTERFLY

Doug and I met in unusual circumstances. I was with another couple friends at a social gathering, as was he and a guy friend of his. We spoke briefly as we were introduced by someone that knew my friends and his. I couldn't help but notice he was looking at me as if he was interested in me. I have to admit I was returning the look. He said something about seeing me again, but it wasn't direct enough. Kinda like a hushed comment during the conversation among all of us. Brief as it was.

About a week later, my girl friend and I were getting ready to go somewhere for a bite to eat, and Doug was coming down a hallway toward us. Normally I'm not someone who speaks to others easily. He stopped a short distance from us and my friend asked.

"Were you coming to see one of us?"

He passed us by, and as we watched him moving on down the hallway, he said. "Well, yes but it doesn't matter. You're busy."

I just knew I had to talk to him, so, to his back as he walked by us. I said. "It matters to me."

He stopped, and started back toward me. When he got to me, he stood about a foot taller than I. Maybe a bit more. You see, I'm a short person. I felt as if we had known each other for a long time and that we were comfortable with each others presence. It surprised both of us, I think. I'm not sure why, but Doug reached out and took me in his arms. A hug, if you will. I liked it. Which surprised me, because I'm not very used to men. Especially this close.

He stepped back to give me some room, then said. "Carla, if I'm interrupting something I can call you later?"

"You're not interrupting anything. So, . . .so talk to me now."

"I want to hold you tight and to kiss you. But, if you like we could go get something to eat and talk."

"What do you want to talk about?" I was avoiding him, but only because I was afraid to make a fool of myself.

He was silent for a few moments. As if rehearsing the words, he wanted to use. But he said. "Us."

I almost laughed. "You want to buy me dinner, just to kiss me and talk about us?"

He smiled, "Well, perhaps more than just dinner."

My friend, Miriam, who was waiting patiently near us, said. "Carla. If you're comfortable, I'll go on ahead?"

 Without even looking at her, I replied. "I'm good."

As she started to move away, she said. "I think you're ready, too."

I saw her wink at Doug as she left us, but she didn't say anything to him. Just winked. I looked into Doug's eyes and asked. "I wonder what she meant by that?

"She knows we want each other." So, maybe it wasn't just me.

"What do you mean? Want each other?"

His abrupt speaking started with me then. He said. "She knows we want to go to bed with each other."

A spike of uncertainty erupted within me. I am not used to men. I'm definitely old enough. I simply lack any real knowledge of men. My own fault really. "Are you serious? You want to go to bed with me?"

"Are you kidding me? God, look at you. You're gorgeous."

This came as a surprise. Men don't talk to me like this. "I'm not gorgeous. I may be some what attractive, but that is all."

His smile almost melted me. Then. "To me you are much more than attractive."

We had dinner, and then Doug started with me. He talked to me like he had known me for years. Intimate years. After we left the restaurant, we sat in his car. After a few minutes he leaned over to kiss me. I was expecting the kiss, but not a French kiss. When I pulled back from him, I thought he was embarrassed. But, that didn't last long.

"You don't like to French kiss?"

"Doug. I have to tell you. I am very inexperienced in these matters."

"You mean kissing?"

"Everything. Kissing, sexual intimacy, everything."

He sat up straighter. "Are you a virgin?"

It wasn't any of his business, but I answered

anyway. "No, I'm not a virgin. I was married once, for a very short time."

"Okay. So, about the lack of sexual knowledge."

"Oh, dammit, Doug. All right. My husband was mean to me. I think it was because he wanted to make love to me and I didn't know anything about making love.

I was brought up in a very controlled home life. I'm very naive in these kinds of things. I filed for divorce and he gave it to me without any argument."

"What birth sign are you?"

"I'm a Capricorn. Why?"

He smiled. "Ah, so you have a good sense of humor?"

"Yes. Is that all that tells you?"

"No. It really tells me I can teach you how to really enjoy sex."

"Doug. We are getting very personal here."

"Yeah. Should we go to your place to talk some more. Or, mine?"

Now I was faced with a dilemma. I felt I would be safer at my place. So that was what I suggested. I didn't think about the fact I had already made up my mind.

I'd fixed us some tea and we sat on my couch. Doug leaned over and said. "Do you understand where a butterfly comes from?"

"Of course I do. They start out s a catta pillar."

"Yes. Well at the moment, you are the catta pillar, and I'm going to turn you into the butterfly."

"I don't understand."

"You're going to evolve into a wonderful lover."

"How are you going to do that?"

"Teach you how to enjoy yourself."

I smiled at him as I asked. "When do we start?"

"We start now. I want to French kiss you. And, I want you to go along with it. Just feel our tongues searching each others and see if it offends you."

Then his hand came up behind my head and our lips met. I was expecting to be repulsed by his tongue in my mouth, but I was surprised. It became stimulating. I began to kiss him back. When our lips parted, I cannot explain why I said what I'd said.

"Doug. I can't this week."

"Can't what?"

"You know. Go to bed with you."

A broad smile crossed his face. "Thank you for telling me that."

"You're pleased that I told you I won't go to bed with you?"

"No. That it won't be this week. Which means it will be sometime."

We spent a long time talking and in the end we agreed to meet at my place the following Saturday afternoon. When Doug arrived I was wearing a button down dress, plus my underwear. Of course. He was dressed in Jeans and a Tee shirt, but he had a small bag with him as well. When he was inside, we kissed at the door, and it soon became a French kiss. This time I started it, and he quickly returned my passion. When we parted, I asked. "What's in the bag?"

"Sweat pants and a CD movie. I want to get out of my jeans and sweat pants are comfy."

"Okay. You can take them off in my bedroom. Would you like a glass of wine?"

"Yes. I would like some wine, and I'd like to have you."

I had to smile. "Go change."

When he came back, he did not have his shoes on. Just his Tee shirt, sock and sweat pants.

I was waiting on the couch, Doug said. "Put this in your CD player, but before you start it, go take off any underwear you have on."

"Uhh. . . Okay. I guess."

When I came back, I felt almost naked. It was exciting to be this way with a man nearby. Doug was sitting on the couch with his left leg up against the back of the couch and his right foot was on the floor. He'd gotten a couple of my cushions and put them behind his back in the corner. He said. "Get your remote then lay on the couch, but snuggled back against me."

When I was where he wanted me, he said. "I'd like
you to unbutton some of the top buttons on your
dress."

"So you can look down my dress?"

"Of course."

"Doug. I don't have big breasts."

"I don't understand why women think they have to
have big tits. Big tits are not necessary to turn a
man on."

Instead of doing as he asked. I said. "What's this
movie about?"

"People. Start the movie."

When the movie started. I stared at the screen.
"Doug, is this one of those Porno films?"

"Yes. Just watch."

I have to tell you, I've never seen this kind of stuff
before, but I also have to tell you that I liked the
feeling of Doug getting an erection under my back
as we watched the film together. I said. "Doug. I
kinda like watching people. . .uhh "

"Fucking?"

"Yeah, that." Then I reached up and started unbuttoning the top of my dress. I wanted Doug to see what he could see.

When the movie was over, I surprised myself again. "Doug."

"Yes."

"I'm ready."

"Okay. Lets go to bed."

We got up off the couch and he followed me to my bedroom. After we pulled the covers down, I watched him as he moved up the other side of my bed. Then he pulled his socks off and hooked his thumbs inside his sweat pants and pulled them down and stepped out of them.

Then his Tee shirt came off. I was only watching his, . . .thing. I have heard it called, a 'Prick' by some of my friends, and it kinda swaggered, you know swung back and forth as he moved up onto my bed.

As he lay waiting for me I finished taking my dress off, and I faced him doing it, but before I got on the bed, Doug said. "Hold on. There's something we have to do first."

"We do?"

He got off the bed and came around to take my hand in his. He led me into my bathroom and said. "I need a pair of scissors."

I got a small pair of scissors from a drawer under my sink and gave them to him. He took them and pulled a towel off the towel rack and spread it on the floor between my legs. Then he started cutting my pubic hair. I let him. In fact I liked his fingers touching me between the legs. When he was done, he brushed me off and gave me back the scissors.

When he was back on my bed and lying on his left side, he said. "Come, snuggle up close to me."

I moved into the crook of his left arm and pressed tight against him. God, it's has been a long time since I've been this close to a man's body. "How's this?"

"It's a good start."

As I lay there and Doug was talking nasty to me, I felt him growing and pressing against my tummy. Then he said. "Lift your leg up a bit."

I raised my left leg and he reached down to ease his prick in-between my legs. It was resting against the fleshy part of me, and I was getting hot feeling him there. Then he said. "Okay. That's better."

"So, Carla. What do you know about oral sex?"

"Doug. I told you I know nothing about sex, or at least very little. So. Tell me about oral sex."

"Ill tell you about it, but I'll let you experience as well. Not today, though. Maybe next time."

I asked. "How often do you like to. . .ah. . .you know." I looked up into Doug's eyes as I spoke.

"How often do I like to fuck?"

"Yes. To fuck." God I couldn't believe I'd actually used that word.

"Every day."

I raised up some to see his face. "Every day?"

"Sometimes two or three times a day."

I lay there thinking about what I was doing now, and how it had come about so quickly. Then I said. "Doug."

"Yes."

"I'm ready for my first time in a long time."

He moved as he said. "Okay. Turn over on your back."

I moved and as he started to move up over me, I opened my legs for him. I saw him reach up to his mouth for some saliva, and said to him. "I don't think you will need that."

"We'll see."

He was between my legs and I felt his fingers opening me. God what a nice feeling that was. To feel him wanting me and taking me. When he started to push into me, I said. "Doug, take it slow, You're big."

He said. "I'm not big. I'm just average. You are just tight because you haven't been fucked in awhile."

He took longer to push into me, and when he was in and lying on top of me. I felt wonderful. "God, Doug. That feels so good."

"Yeah. It does."

"I haven't been like this in a long time. So, to be full of you is really nice."

"I'm going to fuck you now."

"Okay."

When he started his strokes, I could almost feel myself stretching open for him. And then something I only briefly remembered started to happen. I let it. I couldn't believe how noisy I was when it came up to my peak. "Oh fuck, Doug. I'm almost there. Ohh fuck. Ohhh fuck. AAAHHHhhh. Oh my God, AAAhhhh. . .aaahhh. Uhhh, Aarrgg. . . Oh fuck, now Doug. Fuck me hard now.

After my climax I just fell loose on top of the bed. Then I could feel Doug hammering into me as he fucked me so he could cum in me.

We lay still, and he was still on top of me. Then. "Carla, I want us to turn over. But I want to stay inside you. It won't be easy, but we can do it."

He helped me and then I was on top of him. He wasn't as hard but, he was still inside me. "Doug."

"Yeah."

"Thank you for the good fucking ride."

He laughed. "Ride, huh?"

"Isn't that what you call it?"

"Close enough."

★

Last week when Doug was here, he made love to me more times in one day than I have been fucked in a long, long time. Now, today, he is going to show me what oral sex is all about. I've tried to find out about it, but it will take the real thing to do the trick. I think.

It's late morning already and he said he'd be here before lunch. Ahh. . .his car is coming down the street. Yes, I've been watching for him. I'll have the door open for him when he gets here, and I have on the button down dress he seems to like. I know why he likes it of course. It's because he can unbutton it and look at me. He likes my breasts and my nipples like him.

As he came in the door, he said. "Hi ya sweets."

I smiled and said. "Hi ya back."

He pulled me close and kissed me and I wanted him to French kiss me, and he did. While we were kissing, he reached around me with both arms and his hands moved down behind me and pulled the

191

hem of my dress up. Then his hands rested on the cheeks of my ass. I pulled tighter against him.

He led me to my couch and said. "Sit down and we'll talk about what I want to teach you today."

After I'd sat down in the center of the couch, I watched him sit down, take off his shoes and socks, then he stood up and took his pants off. I was aware of him taking off his shirt, but I was watching his prick moving around.

He sat down next to me, leaned over and kissed me again. Then when he leaned back, and before we started talking, his hand began to stroke his prick. I just reached over and moved his hand out of the way, and used my hand on him. As I moved my hand up and down I could feel the hardness of the muscle tissues in his erection.

"Carla. You know how men like to suck on a woman's nipples?"

"Yes."

"They suck on them because it is pleasurable to both, them and the woman."

"I know I liked it when you sucked on my nipples."

"Okay. I think that women like to suck a man's cock for the same reason a man likes to suck on their tits and nipples. It gives both of them pleasure."

"That makes sense to me." God I liked holding him in my hand.

"Lets go to bed and I'll use my tongue on you to try to excite you."

I didn't wait for him to get up. I did it too fast for him. Was I eager.? Yes, I was.

He watched me getting undressed while he played with his prick, and he told me. "Put a pillow under your ass."

"A pillow?"

"Yes. It will raise you a bit and let me get to you easier."

I got onto my bed and when I was where Doug wanted me, he moved between my legs. He started by kissing me inside my thighs. It made me hungrier for more. When I felt his tongue brush against my fleshy lips, I actually jolted. "Oh my God, Doug."

He raised up some and asked. "You okay?"

"Damn right I'm okay. I like that, you know with your tongue. It just surprised me."

With his head buried between my legs and the way he was licking my clit, I could feel the need to get off. It was climbing up my thighs and I was urging it to keep coming. I climaxed heavily. I have never climaxed like that before. It was intense. Maybe even more that my first climax last weekend. I'd had my hand on Doug's head, feeling him work me as I climbed up the ladder of pleasure.

Doug let me come down for a while he sucked my nipples. Then he lay by my side and said. "When you're ready, I want you to move down on the bed. Get comfortable, then lean over and put your mouth over my cock. Keep your teeth back out of the way, and then suck on me."

"Just put my mouth on you. Just hold you in my mouth?"

"No, not exactly. In a sense you are going to fuck me with your mouth."

"How will I know if I'm doing it right, or long enough?"

"Oh, you'll know."

When I slipped my mouth over the end of Doug's prick I liked it right away. It felt good to have him in my mouth like this. I started to explore him with my tongue, then I started moving up and down on him.

He said. "Fuck. That's good. Just keep it up."

I sucked him, then he fucked me. As we showered, Doug said. "Lets go do some shopping and then get a bite to eat."

"What are we going shopping for?"

"I'd like to see you roaming around the house in something more shear. Something that will let me see your nipples."

"I know of a good lingerie shop. We can go there."

While we were in the shop, I found a nice pull over thing. One that came down to just above my knees. I also found a pair of shorts for Doug. They are a light mesh kind of fabric. Something that you can consider as shorts but lets you see the man inside them at the same time.

We were just finishing the last of our meal, picking at the french fries and sipping the remains of our sodas. When I turned to look at Doug, then said. "Lets go home and fuck."

He looked at me, smiled, then nodded. Then he nodded again and I understood he wanted me to look the other way. When I turned around, I saw a woman sitting alone and sipping her coffee. She has a look on her face that I knew it meant. *"I can't believe what I just heard."*

I smiled at her and said. "He's a really good fuck."

She grinned back at me and said. "Lucky you."

Later, at home and as we were watching another porno film, I was sitting next to Doug in my shear top. He was wearing the new shorts I got for him, but the pant's leg on my side had ridden up some and I could see the end of his prick sticking out from under the fabric. I leaned way over and kissed the end of his prick. I'd liked it when he came in my mouth earlier today, and I knew I was going to such on him often.

When I raised back up Doug's hand moved over between my legs and I opened them further for him. I knew it wasn't going to be long and I was ready for him to take me again.

THE DARK OF NIGHT
Larry sleeps very soundly. I mean, very soundly.
He does wake up when his alarm goes off in the
morning, but he sleeps through most everything
else. And, I kinda like this, but let me tell you why.
I'm a woman who really likes sex, so I get excited
easily. A while back I got up one night to go to the
bathroom. When I came back to beds I cuddled up
to Larry to get warm, and because he was lying on
his back I reached down to take his cock in my
hand. I suppose he's always been this way and I
just never paid any attention to it, but now it
surprised me. When I wrapped my hand around his
cock, it started to kinda pulse, or move around a
little bit.

Intrigued, I put my thumb on one side of his cock
and two fingers on the other side, then I started
stroking him slowly. It wasn't an instant reaction,
but his cock started to get hard. Damn, the idea of
my playing with his cock while he was asleep,
stirred me between the legs. I took it easy, but I
lifted the covers off of his waist and his crouch.
Then I moved down further on the bed. I had to be
careful not to lean over onto him, but I was able to
slip my mouth over his cock and suck on it. Fuck
this was exciting and with the feel of him in my
mouth, I fucking climaxed after a short time. I
dried him with my mouth as best I could, then
moved back up on the bed and covered us up.
Pleased with myself, I went to sleep.

When the alarm went off in the morning, Larry shut it off, turned up on his side and reached for me. His hand feeling my tits, then suddenly, he pulled the covers off of us, and said. "Move your ass over here."

I was startled. "What?"

"You heard me. Move your fucking ass over here."

I moved toward him, and he moved up over me and between my legs. He wet his cock, and more than he usually does, then he reached down to open me and he shoved his hard shaft all the way into my pussy. He never pushes all the way into on the first stroke. He usually takes two or three strokes before he's all the way in me. But not this time. This time I felt his cock invaded my pussy, as if it mattered if I was ready or not.

"Larry, What. . . "

"Sshhussh. Just be quiet. I'm so fucking horny this morning that I'm gonna fuck you now."

Larry pounded into me. Jarring my clit on each of his down plunges. Jamming his cock deep into me. After a few minutes he dropped heavily on top of me and I knew he was cumming. I had already

reached my peak and climaxed. It was different
this time, though. I just lay there and felt it
climbing up to my pussy, then it just happened.

While Larry shaved and showered, I got up to fix
his breakfast and a lunch to take with him to work.
After he'd gone for the day, I thought about what
had happened. I figured that if I could suck his
cock at night, and get off, then get a good fucking
pounding the next morning, I'd do it a couple of
times a month. At least, maybe more. God that was
a good fuck he gave me this morning.

THE SLUT

When I met Harold at the door on Tuesday, I was only wearing a Tee Shirt. That's it, nothing else. Once he was inside, I put my arms up around his neck and felt his hands going down to the cheeks of my ass. After our first passionate kiss, he said. "You sweet slut, you are no doubt horny, so what would you like?"

"Slut?" I was surprised to hear him say that about me. Okay, not really.

"Yes, slut is a good name for you when you are like this."

"Why do you say that?"

"Because any other time you wouldn't meet me at the door dressed this way. Okay, sometimes you are completely naked, but it's the same thing. When you are horny, you act like a slutty woman. So, what would you like?"

I had to grin, and said. "I'd like you to eat my pussy."

"I'd like that too."

I led him to our bedroom, and while he got undressed I put a pillow down on the bed right where my ass would end up being. Then I laid down and got comfortable.

When I raised my knees, I opened my legs wide so he could get to me with his face. My fingers couldn't wait, so while he finished getting undressed, I played with my clit. When he came to me, he crawled onto the end of the bed, and moved up between my legs. He started by slowly kissing my inner thighs. He knew I wanted his tongue to start on me, but he took his time with his kisses. I was so fucking hot that I finally said. "God, Harold, lick my fucking cunt." When I did feel his tongue, touch my lips, I almost came right away. Harold worked my clit long enough to get me off twice. Then he raised up and moved over me and fucked me until I came again.

As Harold showered, I thought about what is was he'd said. Yes, I guess I am a slut. But, it is by my choice to be one. I'll tell you about this kind of thinking, but first let me explain.

I have a routine that I follow, not necessarily in any particular order, but they are effective. Sometimes I will meet Harold at the door when he gets home, wearing only a light bathrobe. One that buttons down the front, and that can be unbuttoned easily. Or I may leave it completely open when I go to the door. Sometimes I will just be naked when he comes inside. I do this so his very nice hands can explore me any place he wants to feel. And he always does.

I started Wednesday off by being naked when Harold got home. After his hands finally let go of me inside of our front door. I told him. "Go get your shower, then come back and sit on the couch."

I went into the bathroom to watch him shower. I do this because when I do he will soap his cock and balls up good, then stroke his cock while I watch. While he dried himself off with a towel, I went back to the living room. When he came to me, I was sitting on the couch with my legs wide open so he could see my hot spot. I patted the couch next to me so that he would sit down in that spot.

I got up and stood naked in front of him, then I leaned over to put my hands on the back of the couch. One hand on each side of his head. He knew I wanted his hands on me. I love the feel of his hands as they knead my tits like they are bread dough.

He always sucks on them as well. I finally pulled my tits away from his mouth and stood up in front of him again. "You are going to give me a good fuck later. Right?"

"You know I will."

I got a cushion off a nearby chair and reached down to pull his legs open. Then I dropped it between his feet. He smiled as he said. "You sweet cunt. You're going to suck me aren't you?" He calls me a cunt when he knows damn well I am really hot and my pussy is probably already wet with want.

I blew him a kiss, then got down between his legs and slipped my mouth over the end of his cock. Harold loves to get sucked off. I'm sure most men do. I like sucking cock and I know it gives him great pleasure, so what the fuck, I get rewarded for giving him this kind of pleasure, and after all he does eat my pussy. When he gets close to getting off his hand will come down to the top of my head and I suck him even harder and faster. When he shoots his cum in me, I swallow and drain him dry with my mouth. Swallowing a man's cum is no big deal, just do it. If you pull your mouth off of his cock before he cums, it's like him pulling his cock out of your pussy before he cums in you. You are both disappointed by the result.

☆

I suppose I've known for a very long time that I am a slutty woman. But. I'm a slut by choice, and as a rule I only play that kind of woman when I'm at home. Well, most of the time.

If you don't think of your self as s slutty woman, perhaps you should consider becoming this kind of woman. I found out early in life that there are women who are looked at by men as, being Gorgeous, Beautiful, Stunning, and the like. I also found out that they are often lonely women. Simply because many men stay away from them because of the fear of rejection, and women stay away from them because they can't compete with the beauty of the woman.

But, no matter what another woman has to offer, whether it is her physical beauty, big tits, nice hips or nice ass. As it is, a man will come home to a slutty wife, or slutty lover every time. Especially one who likes to fuck. Just in case you truly don't understand what a slutty woman is like, let me tell you by giving you an idea of what a slutty woman might do. Get yourself a light housecoat, or bathrobe. One that can be opened easily. If you prefer Tee shirts, get on that has a deep Vee neckline. Or, perhaps one of those nightgowns that are like large Tee shirts.

Of course being naked will make any man horny. Also, a waxed, or shaved pussy is always a good thing to offer a man. They love fucking a shaved pussy.

I've never known a man who didn't like being naked around a woman, so you can encourage that as well. Especially around a naked woman, and one they know is slutty.

If you want to start slowly, invite him to sit with you on the living room on the couch. If he wants to watch the evening news or just to talk while he enjoys a drink. You sit beside him, but that's where the normal part of the evening stops. You see, you should have your hand between his legs, and more than likely, you should be holding onto his cock. Hard or soft. It doesn't matter. Think about leaving your legs slightly open, so that he can reach inside them to touch you while you are holding his cock, he will reach for you, I promise. Sometimes right after he sits down, sometimes it may be a bit longer. But he knows the rewards of touching and feeling your clit.

When you are ready, you may simply tell him. "I want you to fuck me." Or you may tell him. "I'd like you to eat my pussy." Or, you may just get up, get a cushion and drop it on the floor between his feet. Then lean over so your tits are hanging in front of his face knowing he will suck on your

nipples. After sucking on you he will hold your tits
in his hands, or he will pinch your nipples with his
fingers and swing your tits from side to side. Pull
at them and let them go just to watch how they
move. Let him.

You can move to kiss him, then move down so that
you're kneeling on the floor between his legs, and
yes, suck his cock. You may even suck him off at
the time. But it will lead to his taking you to bed
and give you a good fucking time. You will I
climax. You can bet your ass on that. I suppose I
could just say that a slut will un expectantly suck a
man's cock any time, and no matter where he is at
the time. She will walk around naked as much as
she can. She will feel his cock, and encourage his
hands to explore every bit of her at any time, and
anyplace. She will expose her tits to him while
they are driving on a trip, or spread her legs open
so he can see her pussy while they drive
somewhere. She will fuck him in the mornings,
and again at night.

The meaning of a "Slut" to me is quite simply this.
What you have between your legs is normally
referred to as a pussy. But if you are horny, and
really need some cock to fill you, or if you are just
wet thinking of cock, then that thing that men love
between your legs becomes something much more
deeper in sexual meaning. It becomes a cunt.

THE INVITATION
I used to be involved with, Ben. Intimately of course. But, he'd gotten a job offer in another city to the north, and because of my profession, I had to stay here. We were lovers, but neither of us were looking for a long term relationship. Before he'd moved away, he'd said. "I have a friend that I think you'll like." And I did.

But then, a few weeks ago he'd moved back here, and yes I was involved with his friend, Elliot. Ben came around every once in awhile, more often as not it would be unannounced. Like today.

Elliot and I were sitting on the couch when I heard the knock on the door. Even though Elliot only had boxer shorts on and I was wearing a long Tee shirt. Actually it's supposed to be a sleeping night shirt, but it comes covers me down below my. . . .Umm. . . crotch.

I opened the door and Ben was standing there. He said. "Hi, Elaine. I brought you a couple of art books I think you'll find interesting." Then he looked at me more closely and then over my shoulder. "Oh. I'm sorry. I can come back another time."

As it turns out Elliot and I had only been sitting talking and feeling each other when Ben had come along. I said. "No. You're here come on in."

As we walked across the living room floor, I said.
"You know Elliot?"

"Of course."

I went back and sat down by Elliot and Ben sat on
the other side of me. He started to open the books
to show me the illustrations inside, and I never
thought about it, I simply reached over and slipped
my hand inside of Elliot's shorts. As I played with
his cock it hardened and I pulled it out so he was
free of the material. Ben tried to ignore what I was
doing and kept showing me the pictures in the
book. But it was making me really horny playing
with one man's cock while talking to a past lover. I
got to the point where I just needed to get fucked,
so I said.

"Ben. I'm going to have Elliot fuck me now.
Would you like to watch?" I knew I'd surprised
both men and they both waited for an answer.

Ben put the books down on my coffee table and
said. "Damn right."

I got up off the couch and tugged Elliot's hand and
he got right up. As we walked toward my
bedroom, back over my shoulder, I said. "Ben, you
might as well get undressed.

You sure won't be comfortable while you watch us if you are wearing clothes."

I knew how Elliot was going to fuck me so I laid with my head close to the edge of the bed and raised my knees and opened my legs. He moved up over me and mounted me. After his cock was in me, he shoved his hands down under the cheeks of my ass. This left his body weight on top of me and his head on my right shoulder. He couldn't see Ben, but I could.

I like being fucked while Ben watched us, but I had an idea so I wiggled my fingers at him motioning him to me. When he came up to the bed, I slipped my mouth over the head of his cock. God, what a sensation. A cock fucking me and another cock in my mouth. I was in a sense, getting fucked on both ends.

When I climaxed, it was intense. I fucking made a noise like I'd never made before. Ben's cock slipped out of my mouth just before Elliot raised up on his elbows. "Damn, Elaine. You've never gotten off like that before."

"No. I like this kind of thing. Getting fucked while someone watches me."

Elliot rolled off of me and over onto my right side. He looked up to see Ben with a hard on and then

Elliot reached down and patted my mound. "Ben, she's fucked out and won't offer any energy, but why don't you climb up here and fuck her now."

"Are you kidding me?"

Elliot looked at me and said. "Elaine?" I didn't reply I just shook my head, yes. I felt Ben crawl up between my legs, then he opened me and slipped his cock into my pussy. I have to tell you, Elliot, nor Ben, knew how excited I still felt. Immediately I could feel a climax climbing up between my legs as Ben fucked me. Just before I fucking came again, I whispered into his ear. "Go deep and slam into me. Now, right fucking now."

When I felt his release I came again. I very quietly said. "Thanks."

Ben rolled off of me on the other side and the three of us lay there for few moments. Then I felt Elliot's hand feeling my pussy and I felt his cock getting hard in my hand. I thought, *My God he's going to fuck me again.*

Ben could see what was going to happen so he got up to get dressed. He said. "Thanks for the invitation. I'll be on my way."

When I heard my front door open and close, Elliot moved between my legs again.

THE OFFICE
It's the third Thursday of the month, and I am
dressed accordingly. It is close to the time where
my day is ending and I close up the office for the
day. Okay, so what am I talking about, well it's
this. For the past several months my friend, Larry
has come by my office just before the end of my
workday. And, on the third Thursday of the month.
Wait, yes. I hear him coming in the outre door
now. So you just sit back and listen and watch.
Then you will understand why I dress in a dress on
these days.

He's coming into my office, and as he looks
around quickly he asks. "Okay

I reply, "Yes."

Larry turns around and closes my office door, then
locks it. Next he goes over to one of my visitor's
chairs against the wall and to my left. He pulls the
chair out from the wall, turns it around to face the
wall, then he sits down on the floor where the chair
had been. Settled, he lifts the chair up and moves it
to where it straddles his legs.

When he is settled, I get up off of my desk chair,
and move closer to him. I reach down and lift my
dress up so that I can pull my panties off. After I
pull them down over my hips, then my knees, I
step out of them and put them on top of my desk.

Bare assed I move over to his side and straddle him. One foot on each side of him, then I lift my dress up above my waist and sit down on the chair. I move my ass out as close to the edge as I can without falling off, and I lean back.

I watch him to begin with, but he does it the same way each time. His hands come up and begin to rub my inner thighs, and I wait for his thumbs. I lean my head back and close my eyes waiting for the pleasure that is about to take place between my legs.

I shudder as his thumbs pull me open, and when his tongue finds my clit, I shudder again. I feel the tension building as the need to cum increases. It's good that everyone else is gone because I know damn well I'm going to be noisy when I climax. As it gets near, I start talking like a nasty slut to Larry.

"Larry, I'm close. Lick me harder. Oh fuck yes, right there, yes, yes. OOOHHh fuck, Noowww, Larry. Right fucking noowww. Uhh. . .Uhhh. . . Uhh. Oh god that's good."

As I relax, I get up and go to my desk. I come back with a box of tissues, Larry took a couple to wipe his face off, and I take a few to dry my pussy. Then while he gets up and puts the chair back against the wall, I go sit back down on my desk chair. I don't always do this, but I am going to today. When

Larry turns to face me, I beckon him with my fingers and he moves over in front or me.

"Pull your pants down, Larry."

I suck on him as long as he wants, but I know that as soon as I get home after I leave the office, I'm going to have my husband fuck me good.

TWO TIMES THREE

Yesterday Ginny and I were sitting in her kitchen having coffee, our conversation was just wandering, but we both liked to talk about sex, and that's where we generally end up. Today wasn't any different. Well, almost.

"Sandi, you know what my husband asked me a few days ago?"

Of course I had no idea, but said. "Do you wanna fuck?"

"No, that wasn't what he asked me. Well. . . not quite."

"Okay, so what did he ask you?"

A big grin crossed her face as she said. "He said. Babe, you ever fantasize about having two men fuck you at the same time, or one right after the other?"

"He asked you that?"

"Yeah."

Ginny and I had both talked about something like this before. I think every woman thinks about this kind of fantasy at some point in time. "So, what did you tell him?"

"I told him hell yes. But, I think it surprised him."

"So did he say okay, or what?"

"He asked me if I had anyone in mind. I thought about it for a bit, then told him I'd want someone who would be safe for me. Someone who wouldn't blab it all over town, and someone I could trust."

"Did you come up with a guy that fit all of your needs?"

"Yeah. I did."

I waited, she smiled, and finally I had to ask her who it was. "Okay, who's the guy you told him about?"

"Your husband, James."

I laughed. "My husband?"

"Yeah. Now think about this for a few seconds. This is something we have both talked about on more than one occasion. If we do this right, and if you're interested, we could both have two men fuck us at the same time."

I sat in silence for a few long seconds. Ginny said. "I'm sorry. I thought you might like the idea."

"Well, fuck. I do like the idea. I was just planning on how to do it. I'm not sure both of them will go for it, but if they will we could have them both at your house at one time, while I'm busy doing something else at my place. Then the next time we could have both of them at my house fucking me while you're doing something else. I say this because I don't think it would go as well if both you and I were with them at the same time just waiting for our turn with each of them."

She reached down between her legs to rub herself, so I know she likes the idea, too.

"Sandi these guys are men, and men all fantasize about having two women to fuck. Just like we fantasize about having two men to fuck us."

I had to admit she was right about that "Okay, if Danny will go along with it, Sam probably will."

"Okay. I'll set it up with Danny. Then I'll let you know when."

Then last night, while James and I ate dinner, he seemed kinda quiet. So I probed a little bit. "I was talking to Ginny this morning, over coffee, and she mentioned something you and Danny were talking about. Some kinda fun thing. I think?"

I saw him look at me, then. . . ."Well. . . .yeah, we were just talking man stuff."

I smiled. "Man stuff. You mean about sex?"

"Yeah."

"What kind of sexy man stuff?"

He hesitated, but finally said. "We were talking about how guys like to fuck two women. You know one guy right after the other."

I tried to keep a straight face, but I finally answered. "Could be fun couldn't it?"

I saw his mouth drop open, then he said. "You mean you've thought about that kind of stuff too?"

"Of course. All women think about that happening to them."

"Would you go for that?"

I didn't say anything right away. Then, I said. "I might if you could come up with the right man to share me with."

"Well, Hon. . . Let me think on it."

"Sure. Honey. Now, I'm gonna get a shower before we go to bed."

I went into our bedroom and took my clothes off, then started the water in the shower. I wanted to wait a little bit for the water to warm up, and while I did I thought I heard James on the kitchen phone.

More out of curiosity, because of our last conversation, I walked over to the bedroom door to listen. Of course I could only near one side of the conversation, I could pretty well tell what was being said on the other end.

"Danny. Yeah listen. Here's the thing. We have to do both of them."

"Yeah, I know we only talked about doing Ginny, but now we have to do, Sandi, too."

I didn't stay for anymore. I went to take my shower. Later, when James came to bed. I said. "Did our phone ring?"

"Huh, oh, no. Well actually I called to make an appointment for us Tuesday night."

"A reservation?"

"Yeah. I'm going to take you out for a treat."

"A treat, that's nice honey. What kind of treat?"

"Special. You'll see."

So, it's Tuesday. When James came home, we had a quick dinner and while we were putting the dishes in the dishwasher, he said. "Be sure you were a dress tonight."

"Oh, it's going to be classy, huh?"

"Uhh, no. but social. Okay?"

We left the house just after seven, and while we were driving, he said to me. "I meant to tell you. Danny and I are going to play in a poker game Thursday night."

"Okay."

We pulled into the parking garage of one of our nicest hotels in town. James came around to my side of the car and opened the door for me. Then he led me to the elevator. We rode up to the fourth floor and when the doors opened, he led me to a room at the far end of the hall. He knocked on the door, and when it opened, I saw Danny inside the room.

I turned to James and said. "Is this the surprise I think it is? Two men who are going to enjoy me?"

"You said you were okay with it?"

I leaned over to kiss him. "It is okay. As long as it is okay with you too?"

The two of them settled into chairs at the ends of a table near the window. Then my hubby said. "We want to watch you get undressed."

There was no sense hesitating, I put my purse on the table between them, then sat on the bed to take my shoes off. After I put them near the table, I stood back a little bit and took my dress off. Then I walked over to put it on one of the hangers they make convenient for their customers. When I was back in front of them I reached my thumbs inside the waistline of my panties and pulled them down over my hips and stepped out of them. As I put them on top of the table, Danny said. "Oh, fuck. You shave your pussy."

I responded. "Haven't you ever seen a shaved pussy?"

"Only in pictures."

I moved over closer to Danny and said. "See how it feels."

Then while I took my bra off, he never looked up at my tits, he was rubbing my fleshy lips. "Damn, I wish Ginny did this to hers." Then he leaned over and kissed me on the tummy.

I liked his fingers exploring me. But said. "Maybe you should kiss me a bit lower."

He didn't so I stepped back and said. "Who gets to do me first?"

Jimmy said. "Danny does."

"Why?"

"Because you're used to me. He will be a new experience for you. So we thought he should go first."

I pulled the bed covers down on the bed and crawled onto the center of the bed. Then I watched as the two men got undressed. Jimmy, of course, I know what he looks like, so I looked at Danny as he got undressed. It turns out he is about the same size as Jimmy. After Jimmy got undressed, he sat in the chair where he could watch us on the bed.

Danny moved up on the bed, kneeling over me. His mouth sucking one of my tits and his tongue flicking my nipple. His left hand was between my legs rubbing my inner thighs. In a sense telling me that he was going to be there soon. My hand was between his legs tugging at his hard cock.

When Danny moved between my legs, he opened me with his fingers, then when he was fully inside me, he rested there a moment while we both felt him inside me, and he said. "Put your arms up over your head."

It felt good to have his cock in me, and after I moved my arms up where he wanted them, he slipped his hands under my arms near my shoulders, and took my wrists in his hands. He was pinning me there under him. Then he began to fuck me.

His strokes were long and slower than Jimmy fucks me. Jimmy pounds my clit because he knows I like it and it brings me up quick. This kind of fucking was different for me, but I liked the way Danny felt as he did me. I was very close to my peak when I opened my eyes to see Jimmy. As I saw him watching another man fuck me, my eyes must have glazed over, or I lost focus because I came from the excitement of being taken this way, and being watched. When I was able to see Jimmy clearly again, he smiled at me. He'd seen my hips rise up to meet Danny's thrust when I came, so he knew I'd had a climax. He was stroking his cock slowly as he watched, when our eye locked again, I came again.

Danny's strokes sped up because he knew I'd cum as well. Soon I felt his cock pulse in me. As Danny came in me, he whispered in my ear. "You're a really good fuck, Sandi."

I turn my face back up and kissed his ear lobe.

When Danny pulled out of me, he said. "I'm gonna wash up a bit."

As Danny moved off the bed, my Jimmy crawled on with me. He moved over between my legs and I reached down to open my pussy for him. He pushed into me and then he rested himself on me and slid his hands down under the cheeks of my ass. He does this so I won't sink to far down into the mattress while he pounds me. While he fucked me, Danny came back and was now sitting in the same chair where Jimmy had been. He was getting a hard on watching the woman get fucked that he had just fucked. He smiled at me then formed a kiss with his lips and sent it to me. I was getting that urgent feeling of needing to get off again, and as it was coming up to a peak, Danny pointed to his hard cock and nodded a 'yes' to me. I knew he was asking if I wanted him to fuck me again. I was at a point where I had just about had enough, but I mouthed a kiss back to him and thinking of how he felt when he fucked me, I nodded yes in return. Then I came as Jimmy hit my clit really hard.

When Jimmy came back from the bathroom Danny was lying on his back and had me positioned above him. I was kneeling over him and just easing my pussy down over his shaft. I've fucked this way before, but it felt new to me now. While I fucked Danny, his hands were holding my tits. His fingers pinching my nipples, which pulled me up from the depths of need. It took me longer to climax this time, and after I had I felt Danny's cum shooting in me.

Jim wanted to do me again, but I said. "Honey. I'm spent. I just can't do it again, not and enjoy it."

"Okay, honey. You want'a go home now then?"

"Please."

After we got home I climbed into the shower and spent a long time in there letting the hot water run over me, just soothing my tired body. Jim had come in and washed himself off in the sink, then gone to bed. When I finally made it to bed, he was waiting for me. "You okay, honey?"

"I'm very okay. Thanks for the surprise. It was fun. But you wanted to do me again?"

"Yes. I'd still like to, but tomorrow is another day."

I could see he had a tent under the covers. I asked. "Did you like seeing me getting fucked by another man?"

"Actually, I did. It's not something I'd like to see often, but yes I did. In fact I'm hard now thinking about the evening."

I pulled the covers down off his cock. He was hard, but my pussy was not ready for more cock. However, I said. "Ohh, you poor baby." Then I scooted down in the bed and took him in my mouth. I don't suck cock a lot, but I don't mind it, in fact sometimes I like doing this to a man. As I sucked Jimmy off, I could feel his hand caressing the top of my head. I knew fucking well he likes this. Jimmy can squirt his cum almost two feet in the air, I know because I've watched him jack off. So when he came in my mouth, I really felt him cumming.

After he recovered, he asked me. "Do you want to have two men fuck you like that again?"

"No, I think once was enough." *'Maybe'*

Before I went to sleep I figured I'd call Ginny tomorrow. I knew these guys weren't going to play poker Thursday evening. They were going to poke her.

✭

So, it's Wednesday morning and I was listening to Ginny's phone ring. When she answered, I said. "Something I think you should do today."

"Oh, Hi. What should I do?"

"Go take a shower and shave all of your pubic hair off. Get as bald as you can. Then, when Danny gets home today, you should only be wearing a dress without any panties on. Then after dinner, and while he is having his second cup of coffee at the table, go over close to him and say. "Babe. I thought I'd try something today. I hope it's okay with you?"

When he says, "What did you do?" You spread your legs open, then pull your dress up so he can see between your legs."

After I talked to Ginny about shaving, I went to the store. When I got back home, I had a message waiting for me on the telephone. I pushed the button to listen to the message and it was a voice that talks nasty in my ear. "I like the idea of kissing you lower."

226

VISITING

I'm staying with Jessie and Mario. Friends for
many years, and a place to stay when I'm in town
on business. The only real problem is that I've
always been attracted to Mario, and Jessie knows
this. Two days ago, however, things took a slight
turn in my relationship with Mario.

You see, I was in the bedroom I use when I'm
here, and I had just finished up working on my
sales report. I had decided to go see what Jessie
was working on in her craft's room, which is at the
far end of their house. As I came out of my room,
and was a few steps down the hallway, when I saw
the television in the front room of the house. On
the television was the annual Sports Illustrated
swimsuit competition. I paused just long enough to
catch a glimpse out of the corner of my eye of
Mario with his pants open and his cock out in his
hand stroking his cock as he watched the women in
bathing suits, or nearly the lack of them.

I couldn't move. I watched Mario and as he played
with himself I got horny as hell. So, I went back to
my room and closed the door, then lay on the bed
and worked my clit until I came. By the time I
came back out I had made enough noise to warn
Mario that I was nearby. When I passed through
the living room the television was tuned to a
different channel and Mario's cock was back in his
pants, though the fly was still open.

Early yesterday morning, wearing only my bathrobe, I crept to the doorway of their bedroom and peeked inside. Jessie was sleeping on her side and on the other side of the bed facing away from me. I moved over to Mario, leaned over so I could slip my hand under the covers. I kissed him, and he woke quickly. As he looked up at me, I moved my hand in to take hold of his cock. As it hardened in my hand I stood up and moved closer to him. His hand came up under the bottom of my robe and he found my wet clit ready for play. I stroked his slowly, then leaned over to whisper in his ear. "I need you to fuck me, and soon." Then I pulled away and left his hard and horny.

Now, this afternoon, Jessie had just come to and said. "I'm going to the store in town. Do you want to come along?"

I said. "Thanks, but no. I've got to finish my sales report."

"Okay. I'll see you later."

When she left, I was watching out the window to be sure she had driven up the street, then I got undressed. I knew she would take about forty minuets to drive into town, be there for about an hour, then a forty minute drive home. I slipped my bathrobe on again and headed to the living room. I knew Mario was watching something on television. I moved over to the other end of the couch and picked up a small pillow there, and dropped it in the middle of his floor. I dropped my robe off to one side, then lay down on the floor with my legs open and my knees drawn up. My pussy at the ready. By the time I got comfortable, Mario was slipping his pants and shorts off. He moved in between my legs then got down on the floor. I felt him open me and slip his cock in my hot cunt.

Mario fucked me good, I mean really good, for almost an hour, then we stopped so we could look like we were not doing anything when Jessie got home. I'd gone back to my room, but still felt hot to trot. I got up off the bed and went back to him. He had his cock out again and was stroking it when I came around the corner. "You still horny Mario?"

"Fuck yes. You're a damn good fuck."

I moved over and down between his legs, then slipped my mouth over his cock. I had just finished sucking him off when we heard the car come into the garage. I got up and said. "Now you owe me a good licking."

It's late and I turned the light out in my bedroom about a half hour ago. I leave my door open, to some degree, so that if I get up during the night to go to the bathroom I won't wake anyone. I was lying here, and just about to drop off when I heard something that caught my attention. I turned my head slightly to hear better, and in moments I heard it again. I was hearing a woman's soft moaning. A sound of pleasure coming from the other end of the house. I pulled my covers off and sat up listening. When the sound came to me again, I got up and walked softly down the hallway to Jessie's and Mario's bedroom door. They have night lights in every room of the house so it is fairly easy to see when your eyes are adjusted to the darkness

I eased my head up to the edge of the door and peeked around to look at their bed. Jessie was flat on her back, with a pillow under her ass and Mario was head first between her legs. I could see he was giving her some long, long licks, then some heavy short licks. I got there just in time to see her arch up and her whole body shudder as she climaxed. When Mario moved out from between her legs he sat up and quietly said. "Okay. Now get your fucking ass up her and fuck me."

Jessie turned over on her side away from me, and Mario lay down in her spot. The pillow was now under his ass, and his hard cock was high in the air. Perfect for her to sit on. Jessie moved up over him and when on her hands and knees, she eased back and slid her pussy down over his cock shaft.

As I watched her fucking him, I was working my clit with my fingers. His hands were holding her tits as they moved in unison. As Mario made his controlled noise when he shot his cum in her pussy, I came too.

As I was getting ready to leave, Jessie said. "I hope you enjoyed your stay with us. Because, and I don't know why, but when you stay with us, Mario seems to get real horny and he fucks my brains out. So, come as often as you like."

VOLUNTEERING

I'd only been home a short time and had taken off
my street clothes. I only had on my boxer shorts
and socks, when I decided to lie on top of my bed
to rest my eyes for a few moments. So I thought.

Her lips touching mine woke me, and I wanted
more of her. I opened my mouth and our tongues
began their sexual dance. Instinctively I reached
out top feel her, but as my hand brushed by the
side of her large breast it was stopped by the cloth
of her dress. She lifted her mouth from mine, then
stepped back a short distance. I watched as she
raised the hem of her dress, then moved back to
where my hand could reach between her legs. I
rubbed against one of her inner thighs with the
back of my hand, then moved across to the other
one. She opened her legs further and said. "Touch
me." My fingers found the wet lips of her pussy,
and I rubbed them for a few moments, then I
tugged at them until my thumb found its way
inside of her wetness and I held her like a bowling
ball.

She reached up and began to unbutton the top of
her dress to reveal her ample tits to me. I'm sure
she stops somewhere to take of her panties and bra
before she comes to me this way, but, I'm glad she
does.

She saw my hunger growing in my eyes as I watched her pull her dress up over her head, and then leaned over to make her tits sway from side to side.

She backed away letting my thumb pull out of her, then she reached down with her hands and I raised my ass as she pulled my shorts down and off of me. I watched as she walked around my bed and climbed up on it. She moved up as high as she could and I moved down. I reached up with my hands to encircle one of her tits and pulled it to my mouth. Licking the nipple made it harden up before I pulled it into my mouth to suck on it. Her hand moved down to use two fingers and a thumb to begin stroking my cock.. This way she could pull my foreskin down to reveal a shiny cock head.

As she moved down to take me in her mouth, I knew she would suck me off, then I would move between her legs and lick her clit until she got off as well. The warmth of her mouth felt like a very nice pussy suck fucking me and I came with a noisy climax. The wetness between her legs was welcome to my mouth and tongue as I licked her pussy lips, then her clit. She too, is a noisy fuck.

After we had taken care of each others needs, she lay by my side. Her leg up on mine, and my holding her the nipple of her tit. She said. "I have to go now."

"Okay."

I watched her as she went into my bathroom and stood so I could see her washing between her legs, then drying herself. Back by my bed she put her purse on the bed between my legs and pulled out her bra and panties and put them on, then her dress. She leaned over to give me another kiss goodby, and then kissed the head of my cock as well. I knew she would leave the key where she found it on her way out.

I knew she had to get home before her husband did. And I knew he would ask her how her day as a volunteer went. She looks in on old people to see what they need then tells the agency she is connected to.

I am happy as hell she comes to see me and takes care of my needs.

WATCH

At the time I had said to her. "I'd like to watch you get undressed." Now, here I was sitting on a chair in her bedroom as she sat on her bed taking her shoes and socks off. As she finished with that she came over to me and standing directly in front to me, she started taking her jeans off. As she slipped them down over her hips she bent at the waist and I could see down her blouse at the swelling of her tits. She stepped out of her jeans and dropped them on the floor off to one side. Her blouse was now being pulled up over her head, and it too was dropped on top of her jeans. As she pulled her bra off her tits came free and the bra followed the rest of her stuff. Her thumbs came up to reach inside the waistband of her panties and as she started pulling them down over her hips, she leaned over and her tits were hanging right in front of me.

I knew she was watching me watch her. I wanted to suck on her nipples right then, but she stood up and as she did she spread her legs wide. Then said. "Do you like looking at my cunt?"

I was looking at a pussy that had the pubic hair cut very short. My reply was. "Yes. I do like looking at your cunt, but I'm surprised you call it that. Most women call it their pussy."

"I call it my cunt when I'm horny. You can hold onto my tits as I lean over. I want you to French kiss me, and I want to feel your tongue in my mouth and searching me."

I fucking French kissed her like I had never done it before. Powerful and thrusting. When she pulled away, she stood again and said. "Wait here for a few moments."

She went over to her bed and pulled the covers down, then she got up on the bed and moved up high on it. Next she pulled a pillow down under her ass raising her hips. When she was settled, her hand came out toward me and her finger beckoned me to her. I walked around the side of the bed and began to take my clothes off. After I had my pants and shorts off, she reached out to hold my cock as I took my shirt off.

I'm not hung, I just have an average size cock, but as she let go of me, she reached down and patted her mound and said. "Kiss me again."

There was no question of what she wanted me to do. I smiled as I moved to the end of the bed. I climbed up on the bed and as I did so, she raised her knees to make more room for me.

When I was well up between her legs, I began to kiss her inner thighs. It was only moments before her hands came down to my head and to pull me deeper into her. As I started licking her lips, then found my way to her clit, she said. "I'll tell you each time I'm going to cum."

WEEKENDS

I've been lying awake for a little while waiting for
Larry to wake up. I turned over on my back earlier
and found him on his left side facing me. I eased
my hand down under his limp cock and could feel
the warmth of it in my hand. I know that when he
wakes up he will take me. He always does. It's
Saturday and during today and tomorrow we will
fuck at least three times a day. We always do. We
seem to be pretty well matched because I like cock
and he gives me as much of it as I need.

As I lay here half dozing, but aware of him, I felt
him stirring some. Then I knew when he was
waking up because he could feel my hand
surrounding his cock, and it began to harden. Ah. .
.yes, his hands are now feeling my nipples and
soon he will lean over to suck on them. Then his
hand, oh wait. Aah yes I feel his lips on me and his
hand is moving down to rub my clit. I opened my
legs and I tugged at his hardness. Knowing he will
move up over me and fuck me until I climax.

As I open my legs farther, he reaches up and gets
saliva from his lips and puts it on the end of his
cock. Now I feel his fingers opening me, and, Oh
fuck yes, now one. . . two. . .three short strokes.
Each one deeper than the one before and he is in
me. God I love being full of a man's cock.

Larry fucked me until I came twice, then he filled me with his cum. He's had a vasectomy so I don't have to worry about getting pregnant and we can fuck to our hearts content. We showered and each of us slipped on a long Tee shirt. This way we can feel the other one anytime we want, and we both like a lot of that.

Larry helped me with the morning dishes then he went to sit on the couch to watch a ball game. I went to the bathroom and when I came back, he was playing with his cock while watching the TV. He does that a lot because he knows I like to watch him and I know he's horny again. I sat down on the middle of the couch and leaned over. With my head lying on his tummy I was stroking his cock with my hand, but with his cock right in front of my face I couldn't resist the temptation. I leaned over slightly and slid the end of his cock into my mouth. Then I just waited without moving. It didn't take long before he pulled my hair to raise my head off of his cock and he got up and pulled me with him. I followed him to bed. He lay on his back and I mounted him. When I was on him I sat up straight and could feel the end of him tickling me high inside. Then I fucked him while he played with my tits, and it's not even noon yet. This will be a four fuck day for sure. God I like cock.

It was after lunch and I knew Larry would probably do his sit ups this afternoon, and when he did I'd be ready for him. He does these about three of four times a week and he only does about twenty of them each time. I was in the kitchen messing around when I realized he'd gotten down on top of the Persian style carpet we have on top of our regular carpeting in the living room. I moved around in back of him and took my Tee shirt off and waited, timing his sit ups so that I knew when he would rise up and then lay back down. When I felt, the timing was right ai moved up so my feet were just behind where his arms came down onto the carpet. The next time he laid down he smiled up at me. I knew he was looking straight up at my pussy. Larry likes looking at pussies so I make sure he can see mine, and the closer the better. When he finished his last sit up he lowered his arms down to his side. I moved back a short distance then I got down on my knees and straddled his shoulders. I knew he was directly under my hot pussy. I watched as his hands came up to hold onto my waist and then the feeling I wanted started. Oh fuck when his tongue touched my lips I moaned with pleasure. I wanted so badly to cum with him licking me, so I said.

"Larry I'm gonna move off of your face and lay down next to you. Please finish me this way. Please, please."

When I was on the floor he moved over between my legs and started to work my clit again. When I fucking came, it was intense, but oral sex always brings an intense climax for me. After I came Larry moved up over me and shoved his nice hard cock into me and fucked me. I came almost immediately then he pumped me fast for his own fucking needs After he came he got up and took my hand to help me up. I had to hurry to the bathroom because cum was starting to run down my legs. I mopped up with wet washcloth and made up my mind. Later this evening, while he was watching something on television, I'd suck him off. Fuck I love this stuff.

I kept an eye on Larry most of the day, but I always do on the weekends. Simply because we play a lot on the weekends. We'd had a light dinner and I was getting ready to pour us something to drink, when I happen to glance around the corner as I headed to the bathroom before I finished what I was doing. Larry was sitting on the couch watching something on TV. After I went to the bathroom, I picked up a pillow on my way back to the living room. When Larry saw me coming with the pillow, he grinned from ear to ear. He had an idea of what was going to happen next. And he was right.

I dropped the pillow down on the floor between his legs, then leaned over to put my hands on the back of the couch behind his shoulders. I did this for the very reason that I knew his fingers would start pulling my nipples, and I like it when he swings my tits back and forth while he holds onto my nipples. Damn that makes both of us hot. I let him play like that for a few moments, then I moved down between his legs. Resting my elbows on his upper legs I slipped my mouth down over his cock and began to suck him off. It doesn't take long to get him off this way. I think it's because I've gotten damn good at sucking cock over the years with him. I just give him a good fuck with my mouth. When he put his hand on the back of my head, I knew I was about to get a mouth full of cum. It was only seconds later that I milked him dry.

We didn't go to bed early because we had fucked so much during the day. But we did our usual stuff. We showered, then he licked my fleshy lips between my legs and then he just fucked me for the last time today. Well, unless one of us goes after the other one during the night. Which happens sometimes.

After the lights were turned out, I said. "Larry."

"Yeah, Babe?"

"Lets fuck outside tomorrow."

*

When I woke Sunday morning, Larry was not in bed with me, which is unusual. So I got up, pulled on my long shirt and went looking for him. I found him in the kitchen talking on the telephone.

"Yeah. Yeah, okay we'll be ready. Just honk your horn when you get here and we'll be right out."

"What's going on?"

"Jeez, Babe. Get dressed will you. We have to leave in about an hour. And, wear that flowery dress. You know the one I like, and shoes of course."

"Just the dress and shoes?"

"That's it. Just the dress and shoes."

"What are we going to do?"

"We're going to the beach with Bill and Anna."

"But I thought you were gonna. . . ."

"Yeah. I know what you thought, and that'll happen. Okay?"

I didn't have a clue as to what was going down, but I went to get the dress on he likes. He likes it because it is a button down dress that he can unbutton any time he likes. I saw him getting a blanket and a couple of small pillows ready to take with us. He also had the cooler with some bottled water and a box of tissues inside ready to go by the time I finished combing my hair out.

It wasn't long before Ben and Anna drove into our driveway and honked their horn. I took the cooler and Larry took the blanket and pillows. We put them in the back of our car then both cars backed out of the driveway and we followed behind Bill and Anna. The day was warm so I didn't think I'd be cold on the beach. It only seemed like a short drive, but I knew we had never been to this beach before. We pulled in behind their car on a sandy area just off the road, and there was barely room enough for the two cars. By the time we got our stuff out of the car, Anna and Bill were way ahead of us. I think we walked about a quarter of a mile up the beach when I saw Bill turn toward us and pointed over at a high sand dune. Larry waved and pointed in the same direction. As Anna and Bill climbed up the side of the sand dune, they suddenly disappeared. After we got to the top, I understood why. It is shaped like a bowl. By the time Larry and I got inside the dune's bowl, Bill and Anna had their blanket laid out and were getting undressed. I looked at Larry with a question in my eyes.

He smiled at me and said. "You wanted to fuck outside and that's what we are gonna do."

God. I mean I like watching people fuck, but I never thought I'd be this close to them and fucking at the same time. We got undressed, but before Larry mounted me I looked over at Bill and Anna. Then I looked up into Larry's eyes and said "Did you see the cock on him. Damn, he's hung."

"Yeah. I know."

By the time Larry started pushing into me I was watching Bill's long cock slipping slowly in and out of Anna. Fuck it made me hot looking at his long cock and one as big around as that slipping in and out of a pussy. I know I was fantasizing, But I made Larry slow his strokes down to the same speed Bill was fucking Anna. Then I watched him fuck her and imagined a cock like that fucking me. In, out, in out, in and out. Fuck I came thinking of that. After Larry came in me, he laid down on my right side and I had to raise up some to see Bill and Anna still fucking. When Anna came, her hands jumped down to her hips as if lifting herself higher to take him even deeper.

The four of us lay enjoying the sun for a while, then Larry asked. "Bill. You ready?"

Bill replied. "Yeah."

The two men got up and Larry went over to their blanket and Bill came over to ours. I looked over at Anna and her big tits were being sucked by Larry, then he moved down between her legs and started fucking her. I looked up and bill was putting on a fresh condom. I thought. "Oh my God. He's gonna fuck me with that thing."

I was so fucking horny by now it didn't matter where we were and who we were with. I opened my legs and drew my knees up some. Bill got down between my legs and started pushing slowly into me. I said. "Oh damn you're big, go easy."

"I will."

It took him several slow and short strokes to get all of his cock into me. I have never felt so full of cock in my life. After he was inside me, he lay still for a few moments letting me adjust to his size. Then he started his long slow strokes. I came almost immediately.
As I lay there, I watched Larry fucking Anna and when she came he was hammering into her hard and fast. When Bill heard Anna's fuck noise when she came, he started fucking me faster. I came again. Then he pushed deeply into my pussy and I knew he was cumming.

On the way home Larry said. "You know. That was a one time thing."

"Good. Because I can't take a cock that size very often." I lied. I could still feel Bill's cock in me for a long time that day. But later, at bedtime, Larry fucked me again, and I came again. Fuck I love cocks. I wonder if Bill would let me take a picture of his and put it on the internet for show and tell.

WINTER WEATHER

I heard Joe when he opened my front door. He knew where I kept my spare key and the power had been out for two days already. I figured he'd be along to check on me. He called out to me. "Bette. You in there?"

I hollered back at him. "Yes. I'm in here."

When he walked into my bedroom, he smiled as he looked at me huddled under the covers of my bed. I had several extra blankets piled on top of my normal blankets just to keep warm.

"Are you warm enough?"

"Almost."

"You thought about starting a fire in your wood stove?"

"Yes. I did, but I am out of wood."

"Okay. I'll get you some from my place and get a fire going, but I have to wait until the snow plow clears the road again.."

"Joe. Are you warm enough?"

"No. I've been out running around."

"Well. . . .why don't you crawl in here with me and we'll stay warm together?"

"Bette, don't tease me with that kind of fantasy."

"Joe, how long have we known each other?"

"Forever and a dozen years."

"Yes and it was a good first dozen years of my life."

"Bette. I'm a lot older than you are."

"I know how old you are. Get undressed and get in here."

I watched Joe as he got undressed. He was nervous, but he wasn't some old fat fart. Old, yes, but in decent shape. All of him was decent, even the part hanging down.

When he moved to the bed, I lifted the covers for him to slip in bed with me. When he moved close to me, I said. "Damn. You are cold. Come snuggle close to me."

I pulled him tight against me. He put his left arm up under my head and his right arm over my waist. I pushed my tits against him and reached down to pull his right leg up over my legs.

"My God, Bette. You are almost hot." He only said this because my body was much warmer from being under warm covers, and he hadn't been.

"Well I wasn't, but from the feel of you, I going to get hot." His cock was growing and I took it in my hand to hold onto.

"You always sleep in the nude?"

"Always. I hate having a nightgown creeping up on me during the night. Besides it gets in the way if I want to play with myself."

I knew I had his attention now, and he asked. "Do you play with yourself often?"

"Yes, and I have a good toy as well."

I loved it when he said. "Why don't you turn over onto your back and I'll play with you so you don't have to."

I turned over and opened my legs so he could reach down and find me warm and wet. His fingers found me quickly and he rubbed my lips gently. He did tug at them a bit and then let them slip from his fingers. We didn't speak for a long time. I was enjoying him finger fucking me, and feeling his cock in my hand.

He knew how to bring a woman to her peak using his fingers, and I reached mine without any problem.

"Joe. Why don't you fuck me?"

He was quiet for a few seconds, then said. "I'm not sure I can."

I turned up on my side to face him. "Why not?"

"I'm and old guy, Bette."

"So what?"

"So I can keep it up to jack off, but I don't know if I can keep it hard long enough to fuck you with it?"

I thought about this for a fraction of a second. "What if I fuck you. It will be like jacking you off but using my pussy?"

"Oh fuck, Bette. I'd love to try that."

We had to push most of the covers off so I could get on top of him without all the extra weight, but I did it okay. He was stroking his cock when I moved up over him, then I reached down to guide him into my pussy. We both liked it.

I didn't go too slow because I wanted him to get off in me. But I came first. My pussy was on fire with wanting to cum again, but I fucked him until he squirted his cum in me. When he came, he was really noisy. Things like. "Oohh Fuck that's a good fucking pussy. OHHhh, now right fucking nowww." His whole body shuddered when he came.

Afterwards I lay on top of him, even though he was growing soft again, and our cum was leaking out between his legs. I leaned over and kissed him good, then said. "You know. I've wanted to fuck you for years?"

LUNCH

John was sitting at my kitchen table watching me
finish rinsing out a coffee cup. I hadn't seen him in
a few weeks as we live two different kinds of lives.
I'm single and he's married and I don't care
because he treats me good.

I looked at him and asked. "Can | get you
something?"

"Yes. Pillow."

I smiled at him. I knew he was up to something.
And, odds are it would be unusual. "A pillow?"

"Please."

When I came back from my bedroom with the
pillow, I found he had moved my kitchen table to a
different place. Now he had three chairs at one end
of the table. One at each corner and one in the
center. He took the pillow and put it on the farther
end away from the chairs, then said. "Now my
love, if you will get undressed and sit right here on
the end of the table I'll try to make you happy."

As I got undressed and as he watched me doing so,
he too took his clothes off as well. He had me sit
on the edge of the table and put my feet on the
chairs. One on each side.

As John helped my lay back so that my head was resting on the pillow, I began to get wet. He was going to fuck me right here on my table.

As John sat on the center chair he lowered his mouth to my lips, then licked me for a few moments. Then he stood and pushed into me. I'll never have another meal at this table without thinking of how I climaxed with his stiff member filling my pussy right here.

www.ingramcontent.com/pod-product-compliance
Lightning Source LLC
Chambersburg PA
CBHW071706030726
47592CB00014B/2092